Orion's Kiss

Claire Luana

*T*oday is the day my sister is going to die. I know I can't stop it. But I have to try.

"Want some toast, sweetie?" My mom asks as I come downstairs. She's wearing her work clothes—burgundy slacks and a black cowl neck sweater, but her feet are bare and her red curls are still damp around her shoulders.

I paste a half-hearted smile on my face. "We have any cinnamon raisin left?"

"One or two?" she asks from behind the refrigerator door.

"One," I respond, plopping onto a stool on the other side of the kitchen island. I'm not sure my churning stomach will put up with even one piece, but if I refuse breakfast, the questions will start. The motherly concern. I can't handle that right now.

Mom pops the bread into the toaster and retrieves her cup of coffee. "Not sure how you stand that stuff. Raisins." She shudders, smiling as she takes a sip.

"I'm in it for the cinnamon swirl," I say. "I tolerate the raisins."

She cocks her head at me, and I know my acting hasn't

been good enough. I'm not a very good liar. She comes around the island and brushes a lock of brown hair off my forehead. "You all right?"

I stifle a sigh. I don't want to talk about it. I don't want her to go all Freud on me and try to make it better. "Just another bad dream."

Cue mother-therapist concern. "Want to talk about it?"

I shake my head. "I don't really remember it," I lie.

Her green eyes search my face and I adopt what I hope is my most sincere expression.

It seems to work. Mom nods. "Well, if you remember anything and want to talk, you know where to find me."

Right. Like my mom being the school psychologist isn't embarrassing enough, I want to be seen in her office? I don't think so. Besides, she can't help me with this. No one can. Well, maybe Zoe could.

The toaster dings and I'm grateful for it.

I grab my toast and head back up to my room.

"We leave in fifteen," Mom calls after me.

"'Kay!" I holler, pounding up the stairs and sagging against my closed door. The vision plays over and over in my head. It's always strongest when it first comes. Right now, it's screaming at me—*Do something! Stop this! Fix this!*—but I can't. The vision knows it, and I know it. I've tried so many times before. Tried and failed. Sometimes I think all I am is the failures, and the rest of this life is the dream. My throat tightens and I fight back tears. Stupid teenage body with stupid teenage hormones. *Inconvenient* is an understatement. I take a deep breath and blow it out slowly.

I realize I'm getting ahead of myself. To explain every-thing, I should go back to the beginning. Way, *way* back.

My name's Meriah Carmichael. Or it least it is in this lifetime.

Once upon a time, my name was Merope. And I wasn't

human. I was half-nymph, half-Titan. I know, I know. It sounds crazy-pants. But sometimes the craziest stories are the ones that are true.

You don't really need to know the whole sordid history. The short version: I was the youngest of seven sisters. Our father was a Titan named Atlas. You've probably heard of him—you know, the one who holds up the Earth? Well, that fun little task was a punishment meted out by Zeus, the god of the Olympians, after he defeated the Titans in an epic war. One of my sisters got the crazy idea to free dear old Dad from his eternal punishment, but things went sideways. Instead of freeing our father, my sisters and I got ourselves cursed.

"Five-minute warning!" Mom calls up from below.

"Crap!" How did ten minutes pass already? I fly about my room, shoving my homework into my backpack, grabbing socks and my ratty but insanely-comfy Chuck Taylors. Mom tried to donate them to Goodwill once, but I rescued them from the bag. I keep a close eye on them now.

I'm sitting on the bench by the garage door tying the laces when Mom appears, her purse in hand. She looks surprised to see me here on time but quickly recovers. I may… usually…be late. "Lunch?" she asks.

"I'll grab something with Zoe," I say.

"Money?"

I hold my hand out and she rummages around in her huge purse before pulling out a ten. I don't know how she finds anything in there. It's like a black hole.

I open the door and she grabs my fleece off one of the hooks. "Coat."

I take it. It's halfway through April; I definitely don't need a coat. But it's not worth the argument. What is it about adults and staying warm? You'd think I was headed out on the Lewis and Clark Expedition for all the gear she thinks I need to bring.

We back out of the garage and head towards Summit High School, where Mom works and I'm a junior. The orderly green streets of Bend, Oregon slide by. I rest my forehead against the window. Where was I…?

Oh, yeah. The curse. The most frustrating part of this all (and trust me, there are some insanely frustrating parts) is that I don't really know how we got cursed. I got knocked out in the struggle, and when I came to, my sisters were gone. So were Zeus and his bodyguard, Orion. I was alone. The only sign of my sisters was a new constellation in the sky. The Pleiades. Well, two new constellations. Because for some reason, Orion ended up there too.

My fellow nymphs told me that Zeus had sent their bodies up to the sky so they couldn't meddle anymore. That made some sort of sense to me. Olympians did whatever the hell they wanted, after all.

I missed my sisters something fierce for the first few years, but Ancient Greece is a pretty interesting place and eventually I moved on. I got married. That was a disaster. Tell you about it later. I had kids, which was pretty cool, actually. I grew old. I died.

And then things got weird.

We pull into the parking lot. "Dad and I have drinks and then dinner at the Robinsons tonight, remember?" Mom says. "Can you get a ride home from practice with Zoe?"

I nod. I can't keep track of the workings of my parents' busy social lives. But it's fine. Better than fine. It means pizza for dinner, then I don't have to explain where I'm headed. Because I have plans tonight too. I have to try to save my sister's life.

"I can get a ride." Then a thought occurs to me. "You'll have the car?" We only have one car in our family because my parents are all about trying to reduce their carbon footprint. It means my dad rides his bike to work and I'm basically the only person in the whole junior class without wheels. But yay, saving the planet!

"I'm heading straight over to your dad's office to pick him up," Mom says as we get out of the car. "You need to go somewhere tonight?"

I shrug. "Maybe just to Zoe's. It's fine." If I can't get a ride with Zoe tonight, I'll have to take my bike.

"Have a great day today." Mom tries to pull me in for a kiss on the head. I shy away. She knows the rules; I laid them down freshman year. No public displays of motherly affection at school.

"You too," I manage, then I head towards the library. Mom has to get to school forty-five minutes before class starts, so that means I do too. I try not to think about how life-changing forty-five extra minutes of sleep every day would be.

I plunk down at my usual table nestled in the back of the school library. Sometimes I study in the morning, but most days I just read comics or zone out.

Today my mind flits back to the past. You need the rest of the story. Sorry, even the quick version isn't very quick. After I died, I…was born again. Reincarnated. The ancient Greeks don't really believe in that stuff—we all thought you crossed the River Styx and went to Tartarus to hang with Hades and Persephone for eternity. But, surprise! Reincarnation.

I didn't remember who I was right away. It was when I turned twelve, maybe thirteen (this was a long time ago, it's all pretty fuzzy) that I started having the dreams. But they weren't really dreams. They were visions of the past. Of my past life as Merope. And then I started having visions of the future. Oh, did I forget to mention? I'm a seer. That's important.

I started seeing these visions of the future. Of my sisters. It turns out I wasn't the only one who had been reincarnated. I was crazy excited at first. My sisters' bodies may have been turned into stars, but somehow, their spirits lived on. But someone else had been reborn too. Orion. If Zeus was a mob boss, Orion was his hit man. Except with a bow and arrow, not a Tommy gun. I was less excited about Orion turning up. As you might imagine.

My visions turned dark. I started seeing my sisters—dying. I started seeing Orion killing them.

And kill them he did. Every last one of them. I tried to get to them before he did, but I couldn't. It's like the Fates placed stumbling blocks in my path every step of the way. The Fates—those three crusty old ladies are up there on Olympus with their loom of souls weaving the cloth of all of our messed-up lives. I'm seriously pissed at those bitches.

But Orion didn't kill me. He didn't even try. I don't know why. So I mourned and grieved. Married, had children. And died.

And then it started again.

And again.

And again.

So many *agains*.

Which brings us to now. To today. To one more chance for me to stop that bastard before he kills again, before he strikes down some poor innocent girl who doesn't even realize she has the misfortune of being the reincarnated version of a cursed ancient nymph. Who doesn't realize today is her last day on Earth.

I stare down at my unopened notebook on the table before me, trying to shove down the anger and helplessness that always war within me on a day like today. I tell myself that today will be different. But I know, deep down, that it's not true. I'm not a very good liar.

CHAPTER 2

Zoe finds me at lunch. She slides into the seat across from me, her face bright with excitement. Though I'm feeling anything but, I play along. "What?"

"Brandon. Cook. Borrowed. My. Pen." She announces it like man has just landed on the moon. For Zoe, it's as momentous an occasion.

My hands fly before my mouth as I let out a squeal of delight. "Did you talk to him?"

She nods before looking around surreptitiously and leaning in to whisper. "He told me he liked my pen. I said, 'Thanks.'"

I lean back. "What pen was it?"

With a grin, Zoe pulls it out of her bag. It has rainbow sparkles and a unicorn horn on the top.

A laugh bursts from me and it feels good in this moment to let my worries melt away in the light of Zoe's triumph.

"Zo." I take it from her, admiring the sparkles as I twirl the pen in my hands. "You're wild, woman."

"At least he won't forget me now." She grins, stashing the pen in her backpack and pulling out her lunch. Her mom always makes her these adorable little bento boxes full of perfectly cut veggies and sandwiches.

"Every time he sees a unicorn, he'll think of you."

She steeples her fingers before her face and raises an eyebrow in her best imitation of an evil villain. "Yes, my plan is working."

I wish I could make my eyebrow do that. I could, in other lifetimes. For whatever reason, this particular body does not want to cooperate. There are times when one raised eyebrow is really the best form of communication.

"Didn't see you at the lockers before first period," she says, snapping into a baby carrot. "You have a test or something?"

I dip one of my chicken fingers in barbecue sauce like it's the most interesting thing in the world. "No. Just…needed some time."

"Mer…" Zoe's face is all concern. She tries to meet my eyes. "What is it?"

"I don't want to dampen your good day," I say around a bite.

Zoe scoffs. "No news can dampen the miracle of the Day of the Unicorn Pen." She says it like it's a high holy day. "Spill."

That's Zoe. She should be in the best friend hall of fame. She knows what's wrong before I do half the time.

I sigh. "It's happening again. I had a dream."

Her face goes ashen. "When?"

"See!" I run my hands through my brown curls. "Argh. Dampened!"

"Mer, this is more important than boys. Even the perfect, the only, Brandon Cook. Do you know when?"

"Tonight," I say.

"So soon?" She looks down at the gray surface of the table, tracing the gash marks where some kid carved *Go*

Storm. That's what they call our sports teams. "I thought we'd have more time."

"Sometimes I have weeks of warning. Even months. Sometimes just minutes. *We* have nothing, though, Zo. This is my problem."

"Your problem is my problem," Zoe counters. What'd I tell you? Best friend hall of fame.

Okay, brief back up. Zoe and I met in kindergarten. We were both obsessed with the movie *Happy Feet*, so of course we became instant besties. I'm pleased to report our movie taste has improved since then. Though dancing penguins, just between you and me, are still kinda my jam. Even though she's a bit hopeless in the dude department, Zoe's pretty gorgeous, with long, smooth black hair I'd kill for, this cute little face, seriously athletic bod, big soulful brown eyes. Zoe's Korean-American, and sometimes I think her parents expect her to have cured cancer or something before graduating. She has an older brother, Jason, who's literally the perfect child (he's at MIT right now studying civil engineering), so we blame him for their unrealistic expectations. She's in like every club and activity known to man—yearbook, junior class president—plus on the soccer, basketball, and track team. I'm on track too, but I run cross country in the fall. The hand-eye coordination thing is a no-go for me.

Despite her insane schedule of obligations, Zoe is always there for me. No questions asked. I won't be able to get through what's coming without her. I've tried to bear this burden alone in past lifetimes, and I'll tell you, it never goes very well. Human beings need someone to talk to. So when I started getting the visions again, when I started remembering who, and what, I am, I told her. And of course, like the ultimate best friend, she was totally cool with it. It went kinda like this: *Ancient reincarnating cursed Greek nymph-Titan who can see the future? No big. What color Otter Pop do you want?*

"Earth to Mer." She snaps in front of my face and I come back to the moment. "What are you going to do?" Zoe asks.

I look around and whisper. "What we talked about."

She shakes her head vigorously. "You can't. What if you get caught? You could go to jail."

"Won't be the first time." I have been imprisoned exactly twice, actually, in past lives. Once in the dark ages (turns out the eleventh-century church wasn't super stoked about my female magic seer powers), and once in colonial Louisiana. That was just a misunderstanding.

"That's not funny. That was then. This is now. I need you. Who would I dress up with for Halloween if you're in jail? No one will recognize Thelma without Louise. And who will come to all the Storm baseball games with me?" Zoe's crush, Brandon, is our school's shortstop. "And who—"

"I get it," I say gently. "But wherever it's going to happen is super remote. No one is going to be around. No one will see me."

"How does…it happen?" she asks.

"Car accident."

"That doesn't sound so bad, I guess. People die in car accidents all the time."

That's true. But not this time if I help stop it.

"I'm coming with you," Zoe insists.

"Absolutely not," I hiss. "No way. This is my problem. I'm not going to put you in danger."

She looks away. "I hate this."

I soften. I hate it too. But my hatred is old, hardened over, calcified like an ancient relic. This is all fresh to her. "It's okay. I've been through this before. Many times."

"I know, but this time you're trying something different. You're in uncharted territory."

I nod. I have tried to intervene to save my sisters in countless lives. And in countless lives I have failed. They have died so many ways, more ways than a human could even conceive. The Fates are infinitely creative. Zeus. Orion. I don't know who to blame, so I blame all of them. I'm sick of it. It needs to stop. So I've decided that this time will be different.

This time, I'm going to kill Orion myself.

CHAPTER 3

I'm barely present as I sit through history (my least favorite subject), Pre-Calc, and Spanish. I like Spanish, because the words float back up to me from my past lives. I always get As on the tests.

My stomach is tied in knots the whole afternoon, and when I put on my gear for track practice, I wonder if I will throw up.

Luckily, after some running drills (where lunch's chicken fingers blessedly stay put), Coach Donaldson sends us to different stations and I get to practice with the javelin. I miss most of the time, but it feels satisfying to hurl the weapon. I imagine my target is Orion, trying murder on for size. It feels okay. I think I'll be able to do this.

"I keep expecting you to yell '*Sparta!*' every time you loose that thing." Coach Donaldson approaches, his strong arms crossed over his chest. His short hair is flecked with gray, his lined face kind. He's one of my favorite teachers. "Everything all right?"

"Just working out some frustration." I trot over to retrieve the javelin, and he holds out his hand for it. I have a blister forming. Maybe I was a bit aggressive with my throws.

"Anything you want to talk about?" he asks, his blue eyes searching my face. He chuckles ruefully. "Though I'm sure you could talk to your mother anytime. Kinda nice to have the school psychologist at your house, eh?"

I snort. "Not as nice as you'd think. Thanks, Coach D, but I'm fine."

He nods after a moment and walks away.

Practice is over before I know it and I'm riding home with Zoe. The air in the car is charged, and the music grates on my nerves. I turn it down. The hot air is blasting, making me sweat, but I leave it. Zoe is perpetually cold.

Zoe pulls up at my house and I suddenly I wish the ride home was longer. That I had more space between me and what was coming. She puts her Volvo in park and turns to me. "I've been thinking about it. You don't have to do this. It's awful to say, but…people die all the time. You don't have to save all of them. It's not your job. You don't even know this girl."

"But I do," I whisper. "I've tried doing nothing, and it's not better. The guilt…" I trail off.

"I don't want anything to happen to you."

I pull Zoe in for a hug. She smells of the little tangerines we split on the way home. The peels are strewn about the center console. "I'll be careful. I'll be at the lockers tomorrow, totally fine, with the most badass story. You'll see."

"Promise?" Her voice is muffled in my hair.

"Promise." I open the door and get out hastily. I don't want her to see my lie. I wave and smile. "See you tomorrow!"

I walk up to the door and fumble to put my key in the lock. When I finally get it open, Zoe's still waiting.

She waves.

I wave back.

The house is dark and cool. Mom left a twenty on the counter for the pizza guy. I don't think I'll be able to eat.

I trudge up to the bathroom and strip out of my track clothes. The hot water from the shower scalds me, but I welcome the needle-sharp pains. They bring me out of the fog I feel shrouding me. I can't believe it's happening again.

I wipe the mist off the mirror and look at my reflection, standing in my forest-green towel. I rather like this iteration of myself. I don't mean to sound conceited, but I'm not too shabby-looking. I have my mom's thick curls coupled with my dad's dark brown hair. I have a smattering of freckles across my nose and face that add to the whole picture. Long, dark eyelashes around hazel eyes. Good-sized boobs. With all the running I do, I can eat whatever I want and stay pretty thin. Which is good, because I *love* the food of this lifetime. I mean, most of it hardly counts as real food, but it's still *sooo* delicious! Pringles and peanut butter M&Ms and garlic bread slathered in butter… Okay, maybe I do want that pizza.

I place my order and dress in dark skinny jeans, a black tee, and my purple hoodie. I'm wearing my silver bracelet with an etching of the Pleiades, which pretty much never comes off. It was a present from my dad when I turned thirteen, in honor of our astronomy seshes.

I walk downstairs to the den and open the closet, where my dad keeps his gun safe. I punch in the code (my mom's birthday—our code to everything) and pull out my dad's .357 revolver. It feels heavy and cool in my hand. Yeah, my dad has guns. He's into hunting and wanted a hand gun for "security." Bend has grown a lot since I was a kid, but it's still kinda redneck at heart. Dad always says there's a bit of the country in all of us.

I grab six bullets and close the safe. Even though the gun is unloaded, I can't bring myself to shove it into the waist of my pants. I feel like it'll go off. How do people in movies just shove loaded guns into their clothing? Worst idea.

The doorbell rings and I whirl around in a panic for a moment, looking for a place to stash the gun. I feel foolish a second later. It's not like the pizza guy is going to come in and inspect the place. I put it on the couch and retrieve my dinner.

An hour later, I'm wheeling my bike out of the garage. I can feel my sister pulling me. It's Electra, I can tell. The second oldest. I was always a little in awe of her. She was fearless and fierce. At least when I knew her. But that was a very, very long time ago. From what I've figured out, I'm the only one in this whole sordid cursed affair that actually knows what the hell is going on. My sisters don't remember their past lives. They don't remember who I am. They don't even know what I'm trying to do for them. Maybe it's better that way. They don't know what's coming.

The visions are like dreams, except sometimes they come when I'm awake. I see bits and pieces—images, sounds, faces. Sometimes I see my sisters before their deaths—happy and laughing—though it's impossible to ignore the specter that looms over them. The fate that awaits. More often, I see their ends. Cries of terror, rending flesh, vacant gazes. This is the stuff of my magic. Trust me when I say I'd get rid of it if I could.

Oh, and I didn't even mention. My visions come with an after-affect. They pull at me—in both space and time. These moments are like gravity to me. Try as I might, the force always wins. It's the pull I follow now, my very own personal Spidey sense. It's getting dark, but the evening is warm. It would be a nice night for a bike ride if my backpack weren't weighed down with a gun. If my soul weren't weighed down with the knowledge of what I must do.

I've thought about killing Orion before—I'm not an idiot. But the problem is that he's just reincarnated. He'll be back—the pattern will repeat. Maybe fifteen or twenty years will pass, but my sisters will still die, maybe even in that same lifetime. Or that's what I always assumed. I'd only be delaying the inevitable.

It was Zoe who suggested that I was wrong about that, actually. That maybe killing him could break the cycle somehow. That if we didn't rise and fall together, all eight of us trapped in the same lifetime, perhaps somehow the Fates would lose their grip on us. It was a novel thought. And one worthy of exploring. At the cost of only one murderous asshole's life.

And maybe my freedom. Meriah's freedom. Sure, we're the same person, but sometimes it's hard to separate this life from the fragmented memories of the people I used to be. I shove down the thought. I'm fond of this body, this life, this century. Who wouldn't be? Cell phones and Instagram and pumpkin spice lattes. What's not to like? But she's just a vessel, this body. I struggle to remind myself. If I have to sacrifice her future to kill Orion, to end this once and for all, I will. I will a thousand times over.

I ride out of the city limits, onto the back road. Tall evergreen trees block the twilight sky where stars are just beginning to emerge. But I know my sisters are up there, at least their bodies. I will put their souls to rest. This is the lifetime I'll do it.

A visceral tug pulls at my chest and my bike wobbles erratically. I gasp in a deep breath and steady my bike, pumping my legs faster. It's happening. It's close. And I'm not there yet.

I pondered my plan on the way over, and the best I could

come up with was to shoot out a tire. Orion's car would swerve and stop, eliminating any accident. Then I would approach and end this.

My mind rebels at the idea of killing someone in cold blood. But this isn't just anyone, I remind myself. It's Orion. He's not an innocent. He has about as much blood on his hands as a soul can. Jack the Ripper's got nothing on Orion.

A squeal of tires pierces the calm of the night, followed by a tremendous crash that vibrates through my body.

"Shit!" I hiss, redoubling my efforts. I'm too late! The crash has already happened! How had I miscalculated? I thought I had more time, that it was going to be well after sunset.

Two cars are strewn cockeyed across the road before me. One car—some sort of sedan—has completely flipped and now sits smoking, its wheels spinning.

The other car, a massive old red pickup truck, looks like it came through the crash pretty well.

I throw myself off my bike a few yards from the crash and scramble across broken glass to peer through the window of the upside-down car. A blonde girl hangs in the driver's seat by her seatbelt, her face a mess of blood and glass. My gut twists painfully at the sight and the smell— burnt rubber mingled with the copper tang of blood. My sister's soul rests inside this body. Is she alive? Yes! She groans.

I pop to my feet and rip my backpack open, pulling my phone out. I start to dial 911 and then freeze as I see the revolver. As I remember why I'm really here. I need to act fast.

"911, what's your emergency?" a perky voice asks.

"Accident on State Route 372. Send an ambulance."

"Ma'am—" the operator says, but I hang up.

I look up slowly, my eyes focusing through the windshield of the truck. Where a head hangs low behind the steering wheel.

Orion. He's unconscious. He's defenseless.

I shove my phone into my pocket and reach into my backpack.

I know what I have to do.

CHAPTER 4

I approach the truck cautiously, the cold steel of the pistol in my hand, still half-hidden in my backpack.

Sweat pricks across my body. I feel like prey approaching a predator. Everything about this is wrong. I should be fleeing. I know how much destruction this soul has caused. How much death.

But when I see him, my feet still.

He's my age. Seventeen, eighteen maybe? God, he could go to my school. He's slumped against the driver's seat, his head lolled back. Blood trickles down his forehead from a gash at his hairline—he has brown hair, spiked in front. He's wearing a yellow and black plaid shirt. His long eyelashes flutter against his cheeks. Every detail leaps out at me and I hesitate.

Can I really kill this boy in cold blood?

There have been a few lifetimes where I've encountered Orion, where I've looked him in his eyes. Always, I'm too late. Once, in Constantinople, the jewel of the Holy Roman

Empire. 1450, give or take. Just a few years later, the Ottoman Empire sacked the city, and I was killed in the fighting. But I remembered seeing him in the market. It's one of my most vivid memories of him.

It was late, and I was hurrying home from a friend's house. It wasn't proper for women to travel alone at night unescorted, but my friend lived only a few blocks from my house, and I knew the way. I had never been much for rules in any lifetime. Our husbands were both merchants who were often gone for weeks at a time. My friend and I kept each other sane.

I'd had a vision of my sister's death for days, but in that lifetime, I did my best to ignore them. It went in phases, you see. Sometimes I tried. And sometimes I was too heartbroken, too weary from my centuries of failure. So I endured.

It was a dark night, but for light from a sliver of moon. A night for dark deeds, it seemed.

I heard a sound coming from an alley—a sound like a moan of pain. I slowed, peering around the corner.

That's when I saw him. He was dressed in the stiff, dark clothing of Constantinople, and on the ground before him lay a girl. I knew it was my sister Celaeno. She had been quiet and demure in the lifetime I'd spent with her, and it seemed she was still now.

For she lay on the ground, blood pouring from her chest. And Orion was kneeling over her, cutting open her corset with a wicked little blade. It wasn't enough he had mortally wounded her, but now he was going to desecrate her body? The monster!

I slapped a hand over my mouth to keep from screaming in fear and rage. There was nothing I could do to save her. Her wounds were far too severe. Tears sprang forth, pouring in hot rivulets down my cheeks, as I fled the rest of the way to the safety of my house. I flung myself in through the door, slamming it shut behind me, collapsing against it, sliding down into a ball.

My servants tried to talk to me, ask me what was wrong, but in the moment all I knew was blood and the wound and the neat little movements of that psychopath as he carved a woman apart. And the fact that I—the consummate coward —had left my sister to her fate.

Orion groans and one bloody hand raises to his head. I pull the gun out of my backpack. I can end it all here. Now.

I cock the trigger, feeling as though my eternity rests on the edge of this moment.

I raise the gun, the barrel shaking as I struggle to hold it still.

Then his eyelids flutter. And open. He blinks groggily and I hastily lower the weapon. His eyes are blue. Deep blue, like the Pacific Ocean on a cloudy day.

"How—?" The word is slurred.

His head drops as he slumps back into unconsciousness.

I raise the gun again, muttering to myself angrily. "It doesn't matter if he's frickin' Chris Hemsworth himself. He's a murderer. He needs to die."

Everything falls away.

My ragged breath and raging pulse. The gentle breeze that tousles my curls. Even my sister, bleeding and dying just feet from me. Orion and I have been dancing around this moment for the better part of two millennia. This moment is about him and me.

As I pass into a perfect calm, a faint siren sounds in the distance.

And I realize what a colossal fool I've been.

"Fuck!" I swear, un-cocking the gun and shoving it back in my bag.

I called 911 on my phone. If the police get here and some-one's been shot dead, they'll certainly want to talk to the only other person who was on the scene. Me.

I shoulder on my pack and bury my hands in my hair, spinning in a circle. What am I going to do?

The siren is getting louder.

My chance to end this, to end Orion, is slipping away.

A plan comes to life in my mind and it's crazy, but it's all I got.

Springing into action, I sprint across the road and retrieve my bike. I heave it over the back of the old pick-up truck, throwing it into the bed.

I haul open the driver's side door and reach over, unbuck-ling Orion's seatbelt.

Once freed, he slumps forwards to the steering wheel.

I run around the other side and climb up into the truck, grabbing him under the armpits and pulling him across the bench seat towards me. It's like hauling a lead weight, but I manage to get him into the passenger seat. I buckle him in to keep him from falling out the other side when I step out. I try to ignore how, despite the blood and the accident, he smells fresh—faintly of hay and leather and night air.

Slamming the door, I run around the other side of the truck, pulling myself up into it. This thing is built like a tank. No wonder he wasn't more badly injured. It must be from the 50s? An antique.

I struggle with the old clutch, thanking the Fates that I learned how to drive stick in my prior life. I lived in Wales last time around. My sisters died in the Great War. Dad "taught" me again last year, but I really just remembered.

I whoop as I finally get the beast into first gear and hit the gas.

The sirens are even louder now. They'll be here in minutes. I need to be long gone by then.

When the police arrive on scene, they'll think it was a hit-and-run. All I need to do is find a place to lie low, a place where I can think of a new plan, a new way to kill Orion without linking it to me. This just got way more complicated.

My mind is racing, but all I can hear is a rattle in the cab behind me. I turn and see a Rainier beer can vibrating on the floorboards, half-crushed.

I look back at Orion through narrowed eyes. He was driving drunk? The asshole. Resolve washes over me once again. Certainty that what I'm doing is right.

We pass a road sign and I slam on the brakes.

Orion jerks forwards, but the seatbelt throws him back against the seat. He groans and lifts his head, looking at me groggily.

Now he's seen my face.

"What the hell?" he asks. He has a nice voice, deep and rich, though it's scratchy right now. Of course he does. Apparently, the Fates want me to appreciate everything about this murdering bastard. *It doesn't matter*, I think savagely.

"You were in an accident," I say sweetly. "I'm taking you to somewhere safe. Just rest."

"You"—he blinks rapidly, as if he's losing consciousness again—"can drive stick?" And then his head drops to his chest. He's out.

I snort. He thinks *that's* the strangest part of this situation? So he's sexist, too. I add it to the list of traits in the CON column in my mind. Right under PSYCHOPATHIC MURDERER.

I fumble the truck into reverse, backing up, so I can take the side road I saw. I recognize it. This is the road to Zoe's parents' lake house.

I pull my phone out of my back pocket, taking far too long to use my shaking fingertip to unlock it.

She answers on the first ring. Her voice is breathless. "Ohmygod, Mer. What happened?"

I let out a rueful laugh. "Hey, Zoe. So…remember how you said you'd help me with anything…?"

CHAPTER 5

The lake house is dark as I pull up. Trees crowd around us, blocking out any light from the stars. Normally, I love the peacefulness of this place, but right now, it feels like it's waiting. Waiting for what, I'm not sure.

Orion is still passed out beside me. Thank god that his head wound was bad enough to keep him unconscious. I wish he had just died in the crash and saved me all of this trouble. Why couldn't he have been driving a crappy old convertible or something? I think of Electra, hanging upside down. They would have cut her free and gotten her into the ambulance by now. The paramedics might be working frantically to save her. But I know that they won't be able to. I want to tell them it's not their fault. There's nothing they can do against the power of the curse. It's only one person's fault.

I rummage around the back of the cab while I wait, trying to see if there's any food. I come across the empty beer can again and my brow scrunches in anger. There's something else back here—a baseball mit and a long, black case. I struggle to pull the case over the seat onto my lap, grunting with the effort. I unzip it, and my mouth goes dry.

It's a compound bow, one of those fancy ones they use for archery in the Olympics. It has too many parts to make sense of—wheels and strings. It's a modern take on the ancient weapon. I look at the unconscious teenager next to me. Just as this boy is a modern take on my ancient enemy. He may look different, but he's built for the same purpose. To kill.

I lick my parched lips as I zip the case back up, throwing open the door and stumbling out. I heave the case to the ground and suck in air, putting my hands on my knees. If I had any doubt whether this was the right person, the bow dashed it. This is Orion all right.

I look down the path to the dock, jutting onto the still surface of the lake. I look back at Orion. He's unconscious. I could throw him in the lake. Drown him. I look from the truck back to the lake, gauging the distance. It's at least two hundred yards. I'm not sure if I could drag his body all the way by myself. And what if he wakes up? I need to wait for Zoe.

It's moments like this where I wish the weight of my past lives could have passed to me as wisdom. That I could be some wise zen master who had figured it all out ten lifetimes ago. But that's not how it works. Every lifetime I start at square one. The egotism of childhood, the awkwardness of puberty, the hormonal rollercoaster of adolescence. The memories aren't a shortcut, no matter how much I wished they were. I have to fumble through life just like the rest of you.

Headlights flicker through tree trunks up the road and I straighten.

Zoe's Volvo appears and she parks behind Orion's truck. She bounds out of the car, running down to me. Her long hair is up in a bun, and she's wearing dark yoga pants, UGGS, and a black puffy Patagonia coat. She's dressed like she's ready for a burglary in the Arctic—like I said, she's always cold. But her eyes are bright and shining. Clearly, this is the most exciting thing that's happened to Zoe in some time. I can't bring myself to dampen her enthusiasm. To tell her this isn't some Hollywood movie. This is coldblooded murder. And we'll never be the same.

I'm suddenly struck by the urge to tell her to turn around. To get out of here before she becomes so wrapped up in this that she can't extricate herself. Before the curse ruins her life, too. But I don't know what the hell I'm doing, and I need her. So I do the cowardly thing and let her stay.

The driver's side door of the truck is ajar and she pokes her head in, examining our enemy.

She looks back at me with surprise. "He's young," she says in an exaggerated stage whisper. "Our age?"

I nod.

She looks back at Orion, then me. "And cute!"

"I hadn't noticed."

"Liar."

"He killed my sister."

Her face pales. "Did she…?"

I shake my head. "She was alive when I left her. But they never make it."

"What do you want to do?"

"Get him inside the cabin," I say, sharing the rickety plan that has been coming together in my mind. It's become painfully clear to me that I don't know how to kill someone and get away with it. I guess I hadn't really thought it through. I need to do some more googling before I can get this done. I need time.

Zoe, blessedly loyal bestie that she is, doesn't ask questions. "Okay." She runs up to the front porch, rummages underneath a flower pot, and retrieves the key. In a flash she's inside, turning on the porch lights. I look from Orion to the cabin in a moment of indecision before running up the steps and into the house. It's cold inside, and musty, but it's still the cabin I remember, with the scratchy Pendleton wool blanket thrown over the couch and the corny plaque announcing "Life is better at the Lake" next to the front door. The inside is warm wood panels and tall beams and is one of my favorite places. Now I'm bringing him here.

I pull a dining room chair out from the table and place it in the center of the living room. "Do you have any rope?"

"You want to tie him up?" Zoe asks, taking my meaning.

"Just until I figure out what to do with him."

"I thought you were going to…you know…" She trails off.

"I need to figure out a way to do it without tracing it back to me," I admit. "I was a complete moron and called 911 when I got onto the scene of the accident. I couldn't do it with them knowing I was there."

Zoe nods, as if that perfectly explains this mad situation. "The garage."

She disappears into the garage and I head back into the yard, to keep an eye on our captive. When he's quiet and still like this, he doesn't look like a threat. He looks…peaceful. I wonder what his name is in this lifetime, and so I creep around the truck and open the passenger side door, and then the glove box. It creaks loudly as it falls open and I cringe, looking back at Orion. He hasn't stirred. People die from concussions, right? That would be convenient. But his chest is still rising and falling evenly. He's definitely still alive. For now.

I shove aside a little paper bag and pull out an insurance card for the truck and see his name. Ryan Kearney. I shake my head. "Original," I say to him. Though I suppose that's not entirely fair, as he didn't choose "Ryan" any more than I chose "Meriah."

Zoe emerges and comes to stand next to me. "I found

some ropes and a chain and stuff we use for the boat and the wakeboard. Think it'll hold?"

"Totes," I say with more conviction than I feel. I suck in a deep breath. "Help me carry him?"

Zoe offers me a too-wide grin that's all teeth. "Thought you'd never ask."

We decide that I'll take his upper body since I'm slightly taller and stronger (though not by much—I'm only 5'3 to Zoe's 5'2), and Zoe will take his feet. She unbuckles the seatbelt and we kinda *tip* him over into my arms.

I stagger under the weight and almost fall on my ass, but I manage to catch myself.

I hook my elbows under his armpits and Zoe grabs his feet. "Ready?" I ask.

She nods with determination.

Slowly, step by wobbly step, we carry him towards the cabin.

An unconscious body is heavy. I mean, I took weight training for PE two different semesters, but Orion—excuse me—*Ryan*, feels like he weighs a thousand pounds. And then there's the fact that his warm body is nestled against mine. I'm hyper-aware of the softness of his shirt, the brush of his hair against my cheek. It's far too intimate for my taste. I want to know nothing of this soul—not the sound of his voice, or the way he smells, or the way he looks when he's sleeping. Now I know all of these things, and I can't unknow them. I fear that the more I know about him, the more human he seems, and the harder it's going to be for me to do what I must. Hopefully, he'll wake up after we get him tied down and turn out to be a total asshole.

It's touch-and-go getting him up the four stairs to the front porch, but through sheer force of girl strength, Zoe and I manage it.

When we finally get him maneuvered and deposited in the chair, we both collapse to the ground with relief.

Ryan starts to topple forwards and I grab his collar to stop his momentum.

"Does this boy eat rocks?" Zoe asks, panting with her eyes closed.

"Seriously." I grab the rope Zoe has piled on the living room floor.

A groan escapes Ryan's mouth and Zoe and I look at each other with wide-eyed alarm.

"Hurry!" I cry, and we begin to tie him—his feet, his hands, his chest. His head lifts slowly, and my breath catches in my throat.

We are done.

I come around before him and grab Zoe's hand in a death grip as he blinks, then opens his eyes.

"Where am I?"

CHAPTER 6

Zoe and I freeze like two deer in the headlights. I knew, logically, that he would wake up at some point, but still I'm not prepared. In all the lifetimes Orion's and my souls have danced this macabre little waltz, I have never once stood before him and looked him right in the eye. Does his soul recognize mine?

Ryan's head is swiveling around now, his gaze focusing on the details of the room. The knotty wood paneling and cheerful plaid pillows, the stack of well-loved board games on the shelf in the corner. The darkness beyond the windows. The two girls before him. "Where am I?" he repeats, those sea-blue eyes fixing on mine.

He tries to stand up and realizes his predicament. He looks down, testing the ropes, yanking against them, putting up a frantic little struggle. "What the hell?" He looks back at us, accusing. "What the hell is going on? Who are you?"

Zoe and I look at each other.

"Thelma and Louise," she blurts out. Smart, not giving him our real names. Though he's seen our faces. Not that it'll matter since I'm going to kill him.

"Thelma and Louise?" he repeats, but it sounds mocking. "You know what happen to them at the end of the movie, right? They die."

Fair point. Perhaps we should have chosen a less doomed moniker.

He goes on. "What is this, some Summit cheerleader hazing? Kidnap a guy? You gonna draw hearts on me with lipstick and take pictures for your Insta feeds?"

"Not exactly," I say. I sound aloof. In charge. My voice doesn't betray how my knees are shaking, how my heart feels like it'll rip out of my chest from beating too fast. I'm grateful.

"Let me go," he says, straining again against the ropes. I hope our knots hold. He looks pretty strong. Solidly built. "I don't care why you did it, just let me go, and I'm out of here. I won't report you or tell anyone. It'll be like it never happened."

"We can't let you go. I'm sorry."

"You can't just keep me here forever," he counters.

"No," I agree.

That seems to sober him up. He looks between us warily. "Then tell me." Ryan's tone softens. "Please."

Zo and I exchange another glance. I guess it's only fair that he knows why he's being kept here. That this is about more than high school hazing or social media shenanigans.

"You were in a car accident." I can't keep the accusatory tone from my voice. "That's what happens when you drive drunk."

His eyes widen as it seems to come back to him. "I wasn't..." He trails off.

"Save it," I say. "I found the beer can in your truck."

A look of horror crosses his face. "Did—"

"You hurt anyone? Yes, you did," I spit, without regard for his feelings. Drunk driving murderers aren't entitled to the luxury of feelings. "You hit another car. A girl our age was driving. She was really messed up. Maybe she's dead already."

His mouth opens in shock and his eyes seem to unfocus for a moment before he slumps in the chair. I can tell if his hands were free, he would bury his face in them. "Ohmygod," he mumbles.

Zoe is biting her lip next to me, and I can see his feigned remorse is getting to her. If I'm honest, it's getting to me. I want the angry, fiery version of him back. It's easier that way to keep my own rage stoked.

"We're not going to let you hurt anyone else," I announce. "That's why you're here."

He doesn't seem to hear me; he's staring at a point on the hardwood floor before him.

Zoe grabs my hand and pulls me past him into the kitchen.

"Mer, this is nuts," she says. "He seems…nice." Her soulful brown eyes look at me with doubt for the first time in our ten-year friendship.

"He's not nice," I hiss, though damn it, she's right. It infuriates me that the asshole has the nerve to come across as *nice*. "He's a killer."

"But this is a new life, right?" she asks. "All those things he did were in other lifetimes." Her resolve is crumbling.

"Karma's a bitch," I counter. "He may be in a shiny new body, but he's the same rotten soul inside. Is it *nice* to own a boarding house that it so dilapidated it burns down, killing nine women in one night?" I bite at the word. That was a particularly unpleasant lifetime in Gold-rush California. "Is it *nice* to be the king's executioner and dispatch women for adultery or witchcraft when their only crime was becoming inconvenient to their husbands?" Arthurian-era England. "Don't forget, he killed a girl tonight!"

"Okay." Zoe holds up her hands, and I relent. I hadn't

realized I was practically nose-to-nose with her in my intensity.

"Sorry."

"If we're going to do this, we need a plan. We need to be thorough. First things first, get his phone."

At my blank look, she rolls her eyes. "We don't want someone 'finding his iPhone' and coming straight here."

Ohmygod, I hadn't even thought of that. I'd just wanted to make sure he didn't call someone. I'm a terrible kidnapper. The devil is in the details, or so they say.

I run into the other room, where Ryan is struggling at his bonds. He freezes when I enter, as if I caught him red-handed. As if he doesn't want me to know he's trying to escape. Zoe's right—he's cute. Thick, expressive eyebrows feather over those blue eyes—high cheekbones—the shadow of a beard framing plump, symmetrical lips. The facial hair makes him seem older. I hate that I notice all of this.

"Where's your phone?"

Silence.

I surge forwards and accost his pockets, grabbing the phone from the back pocket of his jeans.

"At least buy me dinner first," he grumbles.

I press the button to wake it up and the password screen comes on.

"Password?"

He looks at me balefully.

I turn on my heel and push out the front door into the shock of the night. It's cooled significantly. I lean into the truck, retrieve my backpack and the keys, and slam the heavy doors shut.

Reappearing before him like a wraith, I unzip my pack and pull the pistol out, pointing it at him. "Password." A sense of power surges through me as I look down the barrel at him. I feel in control again. My relief is palpable.

"Woah," he says. "Easy."

"Give me your password," I say through gritted teeth.

"0622. Jesus Christ, calm down." His eyes are fixed on the barrel of the gun.

I return to the kitchen, setting the gun down on the polished concrete countertop.

Zoe's eyes widen, but she says nothing. I punch in the code, and without a word, Zoe and I crowd around the screen, loading his Facebook app. The less I know about Ryan, the better, but I can't help myself. We're drawn to it, like moths to a flame.

His page is sparse; it's clear he rarely uses it. Occasionally, he's been tagged by other people. Friends. Family.

Zoe hisses in a breath as a picture comes up. It's Ryan and Brandon Cook, sitting on a tractor. Ryan is standing on the wheel. They both wear worn baseball caps and easy smiles. "He knows Brandon!" she whispers.

"It doesn't matter." I keep scrolling. A picture of him and a smiling old woman with permed white hair and a green cardigan. They look happy.

I close my eyes and hand the phone to Zoe.

When I open them, she's powered it down and set it on top of the empty breadbox.

"We don't have to do this," she pleads. "You heard him. We can let him go."

"*You* don't have to do this," I counter, though I desperately want her to stay. "Go home. You don't have to be involved."

"Friends stick together," she insists. "If you stay, I stay."

She pulls me into her arms and I bury my head in her neck, in the comfort of the scent of coconut shampoo and downy fabric softener radiating off her.

Ryan calls to us from the other room. "If you two are done having your girl moment, get in here. I need to pee."

CHAPTER 7

Zoe and I stand looking at Ryan.

She's chewing her lip.

I'm drumming my fingernails against my crossed biceps. How the hell are we going to untie him and get him to the bathroom and back without him making a run for it? Or overpowering us? The picture of the tractor floats into my mind as I eye the hard muscles working under his plaid shirt. I've seen enough movies to know that even with the gun trained on him, he'd probably lunge for it and I'd just as likely accidentally shoot myself or Zoe. Not an option.

Ryan seems ridiculously pleased with himself that he's thrown such a fine little wrench in our grand plan.

I narrow my eyes at him. "Maybe we'll just let you pee your pants."

He calls my bluff. "But then it would smell in here, and it's just unsanitary. I don't think that's the type of operation you're running."

Damn it, he's right. I don't want to soil Zoe's family's cabin. Ew.

"I have an idea." Zoe nods her head towards the garage. I follow her in.

"Are you thinking, like, just find him a water bottle to pee in?" I ask, grimacing at the thought of the rock-paper-scissors we'd have to do to figure out who had the misfortune of getting…things…into position.

"Ew, no. And at some point, he's going to have to do the other one, right?" Zoe says. "Dad's, like, obsessed with safety. He thinks there are murderers and rapists behind every tree waiting to get us." She rummages around on a shelf. "Aha!" She has an item in each hand. One I recognize as a container of pepper spray. The other, a black remote-control-like device, is unfamiliar to me.

"It's a Taser." She waggles it at me.

I let out a surprise laugh. "You guys have a Taser?"

"Pepper spray is for running; Taser is for all other times."

"Your dad is hopeless." I roll my eyes. But it *will* come in handy against one murderer.

I take the Taser from her, examining its mechanism. Seems straightforward. Definitely preferable to getting into an armed shootout. We return to the living room and Ryan's eyes are wary, tracking our movements. I take the gun and put it a drawer in the kitchen, so Ryan isn't tempted to go for it in a mad bid for freedom.

I return. "We have a Taser and pepper spray. Try anything and you'll be in a lot of pain."

"You can't hit me with that thing," Ryan says of the Taser. He looks at it like I'm pointing the devil's own pitchfork at him.

"If you cooperate, we won't have to." I hand the Taser back to Zoe and she stands, double fisted, as I lean down to untie Ryan's feet. It feels far too vulnerable; my mind races over all the things he could try. Kicking out at me, tipping the chair over on me, etcetera, etcetera. I know that we'll only pull this off with Ryan's cooperation. Because he doesn't know what we actually have in store for him.

He offers a half-hearted joke. "I always thought if a girl tied me up, we'd have less of an audience."

"Spare us the frat boy humor." I scoff, moving up to the ropes around his wrists. His hands are free.

Then the ropes around his broad chest go slack and I pull in a breath, standing quickly and backing away, retrieving the Taser from Zoe. "Move." I nod towards the hallway with the bathroom.

He stands, and I realize how much taller he is than Zoe and me. Almost six feet maybe. How much bigger. This little plastic device doesn't make me feel very secure against the weight of our history, but I push my fears down with a vicious shove.

He gets to the bathroom and I realize we didn't clear it for dangerous items. There could be a razor blade or something in there…but it's too late. He's at the door.

"Be right out," he calls in a singsong voice, our ropes still trailing from his hands.

"Can't wait," I respond in a matching tone. "Come right out," I call after him. "No dawdling."

As soon as the door shuts, Zoe wipes one hand on her yoga pants, then the other. "Holy hell, Mer," she whispers. "I don't know if I'm cut out for this shit."

"You're doing great," I say, though I completely agree with her. "This'll be great fodder for your college essays."

She lets out a genuine laugh at that. "Tell us about a time when your character was tested."

I answer. "Well, this one time, when I kidnapped an ancient reincarnated Greek villain with my best friend…"

A flush sounds and a few moments later the bathroom door flies open and Zoe and I both jump, our weapons trained on Ryan. His hands are blessedly empty of weapons.

"That was fast." I narrow my eyes. "Did you even wash your hands?"

"What do you think I am, a heathen?" he asks, outraged. Like that's the most insulting thing that has happened to him all night.

He walks towards us and we back up hastily into the living room, and again I don't feel like the kidnapper. If he ran for it, I don't know what would happen.

But he returns to the chair like the well-behaved kidnap victim that he's turning out to be. "You guys have any food? Or some water?"

I quickly tie Ryan back up again, and when it's done, I let out a shuddering sigh of relief.

Ryan seems amused, which just pisses me off.

Zoe and I briefly converse. We decide she'll go home, and I'll stay to keep an eye on him. I grab my phone and text my mom that I'm staying at Zoe's. She's going to go home, grab some food, and come back in the morning to pick me up. We'll have to leave him here alone during the day. There's no way I can miss school without cluing in my mom that something's up.

I walk Zoe out to the porch and we hug. "Be careful," she says. "Don't untie him alone."

"I won't let him drink too much water," I joke.

She pulls back and looks at me, her hands resting on my shoulders. "If you're going to do it, we need to end this soon. The longer he stays here, the harder it will be."

I nod. She's right. I can already feel my resolve slipping. This guy seems okay. I search for the embers of my anger from before. The empty beer can. Blood dripping down my sister's face as she hung upside down in her mangled car. My memories, surfaced from prior lifetimes. The coals are still hot. I just need to blow them back to life. Stay in control of the situation. Do what must be done.

But when Zoe drives away and I'm left here alone with him, I can't help the feeling in the pit of my stomach that I'm not in control at all. That there's a puppet master jerking the strings of all of our destinies, twining us together yet again. That in this lifetime, the Fates have just found a more creative way to ruin the Pleiades sisters.

I'm overcome with shyness as I walk back into the living room.

"And then there were two." Ryan offers a weak smile.

I don't respond, walking past him to the kitchen. I retrieve a glass of water and wet a paper towel.

"Thelma?" he calls after me. "Everything all right?"

I come back into the room and scoff at him. "I'm Louise, and no, everything is definitely not all right."

I hold the glass up to his lips and tip it back for him to drink. I'm a little over aggressive with the angle and water dribbles onto his shirt as he can't keep up.

"Don't drown me." He coughs as I take the glass away.

I set the glass down and dab the paper towel at his forehead, where his blood has dried. He hisses and jerks away, but I grab the back of his head to make him hold still. His hair is downy beneath my fingers.

"Why are you doing all this?" he asks quietly as I work to clean the blood from him. I'll need to get some Neosporin from the bathroom to make sure it doesn't get infected.

I can feel his eyes examining me, but I can't meet them. I don't know why I'm doing this. If I'm just going to kill him, what does it matter if he gets an infection? But maybe I'm doing it to prove to myself that I'm not like him. That I can be kind, even when I have to be cruel. The thought melts a tension that was coiled within me. Yes. My goal will be to find the kindest way to end him. To give him a peaceful death, the kind of death my sisters never had.

"Louise." The word is soft. "I can't stay here for long.

There's…someone who depends on me. My grandma. I'm the only one who can drive her places. Make sure she takes her medicine. Pay our bills. I have work tomorrow. I don't know what's going on with you and your friend, but it's really important that it's over soon."

I don't want to know this—that he has someone who depends on him. But even murderers have families, I suppose.

I meet his eyes then. That blue ocean deep enough to drown in.

"I can promise you this much," I say. My throat is scratchy and I clear it. "It'll be over soon."

CHAPTER 8

The next morning is a strange blur. Zoe comes with Pop-Tarts and we feed Ryan, give him some water, and untie him so he can use the bathroom. It's like Zoe and I have adopted a pet murderer.

He's pretty pissed when I announce we're leaving. I feel a little guilty, which just pisses me off. I need to be stone cold.

On the way to school, I let Zoe know my new plan. "I'm going to find a way to kill him kindly," I announce. "The gentlest way to go. Then we'll dump his body in the lake."

She nods. "So like poison or something?"

"Yeah, or drug overdose maybe? I need to google it."

"Well, they can trace your search history," she says. "Don't use your phone. Do it on one of the library computers."

And that's why Zoe's going to get into one of the best colleges. She's a frickin' genius.

I wave to Mom as I pass her office on my way to my locker. I feel grimy from not showering and strung out from lack of sleep. A bacon breakfast sandwich from the school's cafeteria helps that significantly, and I sink into my chair in first period history with relief. Here, I can veg out for a while.

Brandon Cook slides into the seat next to me, and my senses blaze to awareness. I've always used my vantage point as his desk neighbor to get all the deets for Zoe—what he's wearing, whom he's texting under his desk, what grades he gets on his exams. Answers: well-fitting jeans and vintage T-shirts, usually Mindy Jackson or Lila Hernandez (they seem to be competing for the starring role of his girlfriend), and As and Bs, mostly. He's a pretty good student. Today, I examine him surreptitiously out of the corner of my eye. I take it all in: his curly, dark hair; white teeth idly chewing on the end of his pen; black and gray baseball tee that looks as soft as cashmere and fits just a bit too well over his wiry biceps.

I'm dying to ask him how he knows Ryan. I can't, obviously. I'd totally make myself a suspect in any ultimate investigation into Ryan's disappearance. But the pull is powerful.

Thankfully, Mrs. Washburn, our perky bespectacled history teacher, comes in and begins teaching. We're learning about the Spanish-American War this week. I want to tell her the textbooks get it all wrong.

I do my best to tune her out, and I find myself thinking of my past lives. They blur together, but there are moments that stick out. Moments when I encountered my sisters or Orion. Marriages, births, deaths. These things are like mile-markers in the highway of my memories, making it slightly easier to remember the scenery at that particular point.

I didn't always know I was the reincarnated form of the ancient nymph/Titan Merope. In fact, until I was twelve, I was like any other girl growing up in Bend. I would read comics with Zoe. We were obsessed with *Teen Titans*, and then *Runaways*, then, *Lumberjanes*. I'd ski with my parents at Mount Bachelor in the winter, hike in the summer. I loved Disney musicals and drawing and Sour Patch Kids. During the warm summer months, Dad and I would stay up late in the backyard, looking through his telescope as he taught me the constellations. The Pleiades was always one of my favorite constellations. It was so small, but I could always find it up there, shining down upon me. I never liked Orion. It didn't seem fair for him to take up that much of the sky. It's like he was manspreading all across the heavens.

When I turned twelve, things started to get weird. I started to have vivid dreams of the past. Tons of dreams. First it was the Industrial Revolution, then the Victorian Age, then Colonialism, then the Enlightenment, back and back like I had the History Channel on rewind. It's like my mind had opened up the floodgates and I was trying to hold it back with my bare hands. The memories washed over me, lifetime after lifetime, strange clothes and languages and faces that I recognized were somehow mine.

Mom and Dad kind of freaked out. I can't blame them. Mom thought I was having some kind of psychotic break, and I went into practically daily therapy. I didn't want to go to sleep, and when I did, it was like I hadn't rested at all. I would wake up exhausted and crying from all those memories. I felt like I was going insane. Looking back, I'm surprised Mom and Dad didn't put me in some sort of institution. I bet they came close. We don't really talk about that time anymore.

Zoe stuck by me, though. I told you she deserved the Best Friend Award. The other elementary and middle school friends I had up to that point totally vanished. Zoe was the only one who thought it was a gift, not a curse. Even I couldn't be so optimistic about it. I wanted the memories out of my head.

Two things changed that.

One. My first glimpse of the future.

Two. Remembering, finally, who I really was. Getting back to the beginning.

I first saw the future the summer before eighth grade. Zoe and I were riding our bikes through the woods, and I fell. I had a flash. It was like a dream, but I was awake. My vision was of a mother black bear and her two cubs walking across the trail in front of us, looking at us, sizing us up. In the vision, Zoe and I were wearing the same clothes that we were wearing that day.

When my sight cleared, I was shaking. I looked at Zoe, suddenly terrified. I *knew* that this was no dream. It was different.

A thrashing sounded in the woods off the trail about a hundred yards in front of us.

We both froze.

"It's a bear," I whispered. "Two cubs."

Onto the trail appeared a black bear. Followed by her two cubs. She looked *exactly* as she had in my mind.

My heart was in my throat. Zoe's hand gripped mine.

The bear's head swung towards us, just as it did in my vision. Eyeing us. Evaluating the threat.

And then she continued on, pushing into the underbrush on the other side of the trail, her cubs following like adorable little puppies.

There was no doubt in my mind. It was more than déjà vu. I had seen the future.

Zoe and I agreed wholeheartedly that I could never tell my parents. If I did, they would do more than just think about locking me away. I'd disappear forever.

In class, I clench and unclench my hands. Remembering that day gets to me even now.

Mrs. Washburn is talking about the explosion of the USS Maine.

It's another twenty minutes before the bell rings. I have a

free period, so I head towards the library to do a little research of the murdering persuasion.

Mom pops her head out of her office, scaring the crap out of me.

I press my hand to my chest, sucking in a breath.

"Mom!" I say.

"Honey, would you come in here a minute?" She's wearing her concerned face, which triggers warning bells in my mind. A daughter knows. Something is wrong.

"Sure," I offer, dragging my feet as I walk into her office.

She closes the door and I see we're not alone. A police officer turns to me. Double crap.

I take his measure in a minute. He's maybe thirty with close-cropped dark hair and a tidy goatee, and brown eyes framed by thick eyebrows. He has a round face, but he looks solidly built. He's wearing a brown Deschutes County sheriff's uniform with a pistol on his belt.

"This is Deputy Romano," my mother says. "He'd like to ask you a few questions."

CHAPTER 9

"It's nice to meet you, Meriah," Deputy Romano says. He pulls out one of the two chairs tucked against Mom's desk and offers it to me.

I sink into it gratefully—I'm afraid my knees might give out.

He takes the other and Mom goes around her desk and sits in her chair. Her curly hair is pulled up in a clip today, and she's wearing her reading glasses on the tip of her nose, like adults do without realizing how ancient it makes them look.

"What's going on?" I ask. My voice sounds small. Scared. I *feel* small and scared. *It's okay*, I tell myself. Better he see me as meek and innocent.

"There was a car accident last night, out on Highway 372. A hit-and-run."

Oh god, here we go. My fingers are threaded together tight as knots. It's the only way I can keep my hands from shaking.

"We received a 911 call. We traced the number, and it came from your phone."

I lick my lips. They're dry as a desert. I nod. "I called 911," I admit.

My mother leans forwards. "Honey, what were you doing out that far?"

Deputy Romano glances at her, a look that seems to say, *I'm asking the questions here.*

She sits back, chastised.

"I was riding my bike," I say, my mind racing for an excuse. "Cross-training, for track. It was pretty warm, so I rode farther than I normally would. I saw a car…rolled over. I called the police."

"Oh, sweetie," my mom murmurs.

Deputy Romano leans forwards, putting his elbows on his knees. "Was there another car there? It's important. When the ambulance arrived, there was just one car."

I shake my head. I can't believe I'm lying to the police. "I didn't see another car. Just the one that had flipped."

"Why didn't you stay until the police got there?" Deputy Romano asks.

"I went to see if the driver was okay," I manage. My voice quavers, and I'm not faking it. The image of Electra's bloody face swims before my mind's eye. "And there was so much blood. I…just got scared and I didn't want to stay. I'm sorry. I'm a coward."

"Why didn't you tell anyone?" Deputy Romano asks.

"I went over to my friend Zoe's house. My parents weren't home and I didn't want to be alone. I told her." Note to self: fill Zoe in on story before Romano gets to her. "I would have told my parents, but I didn't have a chance."

My mom's hand is over her mouth; she's shaking her head. She clearly feels awful that she wasn't there for me in my time of need. I want to tell her not to worry. I've been witnessing horrors without her and Dad for millennia.

My story seems to satisfy Deputy Romano. He stands and

hands me a card. "Thanks, Meriah. If you think of anything else, any other details, please give me a call."

My mom and I stand too. Before he leaves, I stop him. "Deputy Romano?"

He turns.

"How is she? The girl in the car?"

I already know the answer before he says it. I expect the shake of his head.

"She didn't make it."

THE REST of the day is weird. I promise Mom I'm okay and that I know she's there to talk to if I need it. I have time for a little research at lunch and discover that there are a variety of everyday household products that can kill a person—including hydrogen peroxide, laundry detergent, and ammonia. I'm not sure that gets me any closer to a solution to my little Orion problem. They all sound like awful ways to go, and I still don't know how I would dispose of his body.

Zoe has a student body council meeting after school, so I grab my bike from her car and head towards the cabin. I'm skipping track, but I feel bad that we left Ryan for so long. He probably has to pee like a racehorse.

The afternoon is warm and the sun is bright in the sky. It feels incongruous.

I hold conversation after conversation with Ryan in my head on the bike ride. Maybe I should just tell him the truth. That he killed that girl last night, along with countless girls before. And he will kill again. I wonder whether he was always like this, or whether time has changed him. Whether Zeus's curse twisted him into something different. I know this endless parade of lives and deaths have changed me from who I was when it all began.

It all started so innocently. With a vision. It always starts with a vision.

There had been great war, generations before, an epic battle for dominion over the Earth between the Titans, led by Chronos, and the Olympians, led by Zeus. Chronos was the master of time and wielded a great scythe that cut down the Olympians in powerful strokes. A scythe that held the power of time itself. Zeus, as you probably know, was the god of lightning. He lit shit up.

It mattered little to the mortals who won. It sucked, being a mortal back then. I guess it still does.

Zeus won the war, and he and his Olympian friends came up with all sorts of creative punishments for the Titans who had opposed him. My father, Atlas, was sentenced to holding up the sky for eternity.

Years later, my sisters and I served the goddess Artemis, one of the Olympians. Even though we were half-Titans, Artemis didn't really hold that against us. We were happy, my sisters and I, though we felt a little bad about what had happened to Dad.

Then the vision came. I had a flash of a future where we freed our father from his horrible burden. Or so I thought. I saw the scythe of Chronos in my sister Maia's hand.

It was simple enough. Steal the scythe from where it hung in the Grand Hall at Mount Olympus, use it to free my father, help him make a quick getaway to some nice island where he could live out the rest of his eternal days in peace. Easy-peasy.

We barely even managed to get the scythe. I don't know how Zeus knew, but he did. Maybe he had a seer of his own. No sooner had my sister gotten it off the hooks than Orion, Zeus's bodyguard/hitman/fixer, showed up, blocking the doorway with his stupid bow and arrow pointed at Maia's heart.

We all froze. Zeus appeared behind us with half a dozen Olympian guards. We were trapped.

"Give me the scythe," Zeus demanded.

I could tell Maia was going to do no such thing. She wasn't going down without a fight. We were half-Titans, after all.

But Zeus was playing for keeps. "Throw down the scythe," he repeated, "or Orion will kill every one of your sisters, starting with the youngest." Yeah, he was talking about me—I was the youngest.

Maia's eyes blazed with fury but she dropped the scythe with a clatter. Zeus seized it, then nodded to Orion.

Pain exploded through my shoulder. I looked down, trying to make sense of it. I was surprised to find the dark shaft of an arrow protruding from my white linen dress.

Have I mentioned? Orion's a dick.

Then all hell broke loose. Electra lunged at Orion, trying to knock him out of the way (told you she was the feisty one).

I collapsed to the floor, my vision blurring. As my head *thunked* to the cool marble, I saw sandaled feet—shuffling, struggling, fighting.

And then blackness took me.

I get off my bike, leaning it against the front porch of the cabin. That's part of the problem with all of this. I don't even know *how* we got cursed. When I woke up, my sisters and Orion were enthroned in the sky. And I was alone.

Ryan is glaring at me when I enter the cabin.

"Hi," I manage, grabbing the Taser off the cabinet by the TV. "Need to go to the bathroom?"

"Yup," he says forcefully, and I cringe a bit. I guess I deserve that.

"Don't try anything," I say, leaning down to untie his feet.

"Just untie the damn ropes."

I get him untied and he practically bolts into the bathroom.

I drum the fingertips of one hand against my jeans, the Taser heavy in the other.

The toilet flushes, then the sink runs. I raise the Taser as the door opens.

But I'm not prepared.

Ryan explodes out from behind it like a freight train—and tackles me straight in the gut.

hit the floor hard and the breath whooshes from my lungs. Ryan is half on top of me, his hip bone jutting into my stomach.

I throw my hand with the Taser up above my head and he scrambles for it while seizing my other wrist in one hand.

His face is intent—focused. This is his one chance at freedom and he isn't going to waste it.

I squirm and struggle, trying to pull myself from beneath him. I need to get the Taser to his side without him disarming me.

"I don't—want to hurt you," he grunts.

He lunges towards my free hand and his fingers find purchase around my other wrist, his fingers tangling in the links of my bracelet and ripping it off.

He hisses out a breath and I still, trapped beneath the bulk of his weight, my arms captured in his strong grip.

It's the closest I've ever been to a boy. I'm furious with him for putting us in this position. I'm furious with myself for noticing.

I buck my hips again, trying to throw him off. But he's

much bigger than me.

"Stop," he says with exasperation. "Louise, just stop."

A desperate laugh escapes me. He's still using my stupid alias.

"I just want to get out of here," he says. "If you promise you'll let me go, I'll get up right now, and we can both go."

My resolve is weakening. What the hell do I think I'm doing here? Do I really think I can kill this guy? I have no way of accessing the supplies I need to kill him kindly, and I'm not a coldblooded murderer. Not to mention if we dump his body in the lake, he'll probably surface at some point, it'll be traced back to me and Zoe, and we'll go to jail for the rest of our lives. I can't drag Zoe into this.

This close, I notice he has a few freckles clustered together below one eye. A constellation. They kind of look like the Pleiades.

He continues. "I don't want to hurt you. This isn't me. I don't attack girls."

My laugh turns dark. If only he knew what his soul had done. But he gives me an idea. "Okay," I say, heaving a dramatic sigh. "This is getting out of control."

He cocks his head. "You'll let me go? Promise?"

I nod wearily.

He releases my hands and backs up off me onto his hands and knees.

That's when I nail him with the Taser.

The voltage courses through his body and he freezes with a wheezing moan before collapsing onto his side.

I cringe as I pull the device back from his shoulder where it made contact. It looks painful.

"I'm sorry," I say. "I didn't want to hurt you, either. But I can't let you go."

Ryan's on the floor on his side, his eyes wide. His body goes rigid.

I look at him with alarm. Is this normal?

His eyelids flutter shut, and then his eyes roll back in his head.

He starts to convulse. His arms jerk around his torso, and his body starts to shake. The violence of it takes my breath away.

"Oh my god." I look at him with horror for a moment, my hands fluttering uselessly.

Ryan's having a seizure. I look at the Taser in horror. Oh my god, I did this.

His head whacks back against the hardwood floor with a loud crack and I scramble to my feet, lunging for the wool blanket on the couch. I slide it under his head and grab his shoulders, trying to press down, trying to stop the worst of the thrashing. What do they say about seizures? Are you supposed to put a spoon or something in their mouth, to keep them from swallowing their tongue? Or is that just the old wives' tale, and you're not supposed to do that? I can't remember. My thoughts are a tangle.

Ryan's feet are bucking, his entire body moving in a jerking, undulating wave. Tears prick the corner of my eyes.

"Stop it," I cry at him, horrorstricken at what I've done.

He needs to die, but not like this. Never like this.

It feels like an eternity, but I think less than a minute passes before Ryan's seizure starts to slow. I lift my hands from his shoulders gingerly, examining his face for signs of... I don't know. That he's still alive. In the back of my mind, I chide myself for the relief I feel when I see him pull in a breath. If he had died, it would have solved all my problems. But somehow I'm still glad he's not.

His mouth moves. "Mer—" he says, a wheezing breath.

I freeze. He always called me "Louise." He doesn't know my name. How could he?

I lean forwards. Maybe I imagined it?

His full lips part again. "Merope…"

I scramble back across the living room, as far from him as I can get. My back *thunks* hard against the wall and I look at his prone form, my eyes wild. My breath is coming in and out in little gasps.

Merope. He said *Merope*.

"What…the actual fuck?" I whisper. Ryan—Orion—whoever the hell this guy is…he *knows* me. That means he knows who *he* is. Right? He has to.

My mind swoops and dips like a wild bird at the magnitude of this. Never in all the centuries have I seen *any* indication that my sisters or Orion knew of their past. Only I was cursed with the knowledge of who and what we are, the knowledge of our interminable Sisyphean existence.

But if Orion knows who he is…what does that mean? Does it mean he's been doing this on purpose all these millennia? Isn't he…sick of it by now? Does he really still want to be Zeus's lapdog?

Ryan groans, and my eyes snap back to him.

He's waking up.

I launch to my feet and run back to him. I tie his feet quickly. I have a feeling he's as weak as a kitten, but I don't want to take any chances.

I help him into a sitting position and angle him against the couch.

"Are you okay?" I ask.

He's shaking his head and blinking. His eyes are unfocused. "Did I have a seizure?"

I grab the water bottle and offer it to him, suddenly suspicious. He drinks greedily.

I pull the bottle back from his lips and seize the Taser again off the ground where I left it. Just in case he tries anything.

"You don't sound surprised," I say.

He closes his eyes and sighs. "I'm epileptic."

Oh. "So it wasn't my fault," I say, relieved.

"No, it was definitely your fault." He glares at me. "Hitting an epileptic with a Taser can trigger a seizure, as you no doubt learned."

I purse my lips. "But you were driving and stuff. Are you allowed to do that?"

He heaves another sigh. "No one knows. Or no one is supposed to know. I'm the only one who can drive my grandma around. And I need to drive for work. If people found out…I'd be screwed."

"But don't you need medicine?" I ask. "And you could hurt someone if you had a seizure while driving…" I trail off.

"It's not like they happen all the time," he says, defending himself. "I'd never had one while driving."

"You'd never had one…before," I say. "Before last night."

He buries his face in his hands. "I didn't mean to hurt that girl. I was just driving home." His shoulders start to shake, and I think he might be crying.

One of my hands reaches out of its volition and I snatch it back. I'm not here to comfort my sister's killer. This could be an act, for all I know.

But it doesn't seem like one.

"But the beer can," I say lamely, clinging to some explanation where I can be angry at him, rather than feel like he's a victim of fate, the same as the rest of us.

"Some guys from work borrowed my truck." Ryan raises his head, hastily wiping his cheek with the heel of his palm. "I'd never drink and drive. My parents were killed by drunk drivers. Plus, I think beer tastes like shit."

I can't argue with him there.

I sit back on my heels, the Taser drooping in my hand. I'm overcome with the feeling that maybe I got everything all wrong.

CHAPTER 11

"I come bearing pizza!" Zoe's cheerful voice sounds from the porch and I spring to my feet, forever grateful that she's here. I open the door for her and she waltzes in like a beauty queen, pizza box balanced on one hand, six pack of Diet Coke in the other.

"Thank god," Ryan says, his eyes greedy at the sight of the food. "What kind?"

I realize guiltily that we haven't fed him since this morning's stale pop tart. He must be starving.

"Half-veggie, half-meat-lovers," Zoe says. This is our typical split. I'm an unapologetic carnivore while Zoe feels guilty about the environmental degradation caused by factory farms, so she avoids meat that isn't free-range and grass-fed and all the other things.

"Cool," Ryan says. "I'm a pescatarian."

I look at him suspiciously. He's a teenage male. I was not expecting enlightened eating habits. I shake it off. He could subsist on a diet of spring water and bean sprouts, I don't care. "Talk to you in the kitchen, Zo?" I ask, nodding meaningfully.

"Sure," she says.

As soon as we're in the other room and she sets her burdens on the counter, I spring at her, strangling her in a hug.

"I love you too, Mer." She pats my back.

"Don't ever leave me again," I say dramatically, though I'm serious.

"What happened?" she asks, looking towards the living room with narrowed eyes.

"He got free and I Tased him and he had a seizure and I thought he was going to die and…" I lower my voice. "He said *Merope*!" I hiss.

"Whoa." Her eyes are big as saucers. "Did you ask him about it? If he…remembers anything?"

I shake my head, chewing on my lip. "If he knows who he is, and he realizes we know who he is, he'll know we're going to kill him," I whisper. "He might get violent. I can't risk that."

"Okay." Zoe shakes her head.

"Pizza, o' pizza!" Ryan calls from the other room. "Where art thou, pizza?"

"Coming," Zoe hollers back. She lowers her voice as she pulls some paper plates and napkins from the cupboard. "What are you going to do?"

"Maybe I can like…do some reconnaissance," I say, an idea coming to me. "At his house. Maybe he has like a journal or something."

"Dear Diary," Zoe says. "Today's a special day. It's the thousandth anniversary of my first murder."

I shrug. "Worth a try?"

She shakes her head. "I hate to put an ultimatum on this, but the longer this goes on, the bigger chance something's gonna go sideways. Can we agree to do what needs to be done by tomorrow? Either let him go or…you know…" She makes a little throat-slashing pantomime and I giggle, despite the seriousness.

"Deal."

My phone buzzes in my pocket and I jump. It's my mom.

"Why is she calling instead of texting?" Zoe asks.

"I better take it. She's probably pissed." I pass through the living room into the night, not wanting a stray holler from Ryan to clue her in to anything.

I pick up. "Hey, Mom."

"Hey yourself, young lady," she replies. Uh-oh. *Young lady* is never a good starting point. "Do you want to tell me why you missed track practice today? Imagine my surprise when Coach Donaldson stopped by my office to make sure you were okay."

"Sorry, Mom," I say. "I was feeling sick to my stomach. I went home. But then I was feeling better, so I went over to Zoe's."

"Well, Dad and I want you home this instant."

"'Kay," I respond. *Crap, crap, crap!* The cabin is way farther than Zoe's house. Hopefully they don't time me.

I run back inside. Zoe is holding a slice of pizza out for Ryan to bite.

"We gotta go now," I say. "My mom's pissed."

Zoe stands.

"But pizza!" Ryan looks stricken.

"I'll come back and feed you," Zoe says. "I just have to drop her off."

"You're going to leave me here with these delicious smells?"

"Sorry," I say, motioning to the door.

"Wait!" Ryan says. "Louise. Can I ask you a favor?"

"Make it quick," I snap.

"I picked my grandma's medicine up for her before...the

accident. It's in the glove box of my truck. Will you take it to her? Like tonight or tomorrow? She needs it."

I soften. Damn him and his stupid sweet grandma. Though…it does give me the perfect opportunity to do some snooping. "Fine. What's your address?"

Zoe looks at me as we race home. "You're going to take that medicine to his grandma's and do a little detective work?"

I play with the edge of the brown paper bag. "I guess. If I can get out of the house."

I punch the address into the maps app on my phone. "Zoe, it's close. Maybe we should just…stop."

"But you said your mom told you to get home pronto."

"She's already pissed. What's ten more minutes? This might be my only shot, Zo."

She sighs, but I see her weakening.

"Left here!" I say.

A few turns later, we pull up to Ryan's house. It looks like a manufactured home set in a clearing of tall trees. The faded green paint is peeling, and the porch is sagging slightly, but there's a tidy row of flowers lining the yard and a cheerful plaque hanging to the right of the door that reads, "Bless this House." Clearly, someone cares for this place.

I turn to Zoe. "Okay, you ring the doorbell and distract her, and I'll run around back and sneak in."

"Distract her how?" Zoe goggles at me.

"I don't know, make up some sort of thing for school. You're fundraising for student body or something. Or say you're doing a project for history and learning about people's life in Bend back in the day. Old people love to talk. She'll probably just be happy to chat with you."

"Ohmygod, Mer, you so owe me…"

But I'm already out of the car and darting into the shadow of the trees lining the property.

I sneak around back, catching sight of a sliding glass door. Bingo.

I dash from the trees to the side of the house, my heart in my throat. I hear a faint knock on the door and sense movement inside the house. Atta girl, Zo!

I know I don't have much time, so I try the door. It's unlocked. I slide it open, wincing as it rattles on the hinges, then slip inside.

I'm in the kitchen-slash-dining room, with linoleum floor, Formica countertops, and dated wood cabinets. But as with the outside, there are touches of love: a vase of tulips on the table, cute little cow figurines that I'm guessing are for salt and pepper. I find myself liking Ryan's grandma. I wish her grandson weren't an ancient Greek killer.

Zoe's voice, full of forced cheer, drifts from the front door, and I slip into the hallway that leads to the bedrooms. One door is for the bathroom, and I deposit the paper bag of medicine on the counter. Let her think fairies brought it or something. Then I find Ryan's room.

It's intimate, being in someone's bedroom, especially without them there. It's a kind of glimpse into their real self, the self they hide from the world. I feel that keenly now as I take in the mussed, flannel sheets, the pile of dirty clothes, the papers on a tiny desk by the window. Ryan has an ancient old desktop computer, yellowed with age. I feel bad. Can that thing even connect to the internet? The walls have a few posters—mostly pages torn from some sort of hunting magazine—of composite bows, like the one Ryan had in his truck. My eyes widen as I take in a bookshelf filled with trophies and ribbons. I take a closer look. They're for archery. I didn't even know competitive archery was a thing. But I guess he's good with that bow. How could he not be, I suppose. His aim is blessed by Zeus himself.

I chide myself. Time to get down to business. I rifle

through the papers, but all I find are assignments and old tests. He doesn't go to Summit like me, Zoe, and Brandon; he goes to Bend Senior High School. It's not as good of a school as ours. His test scores seem pretty good, though. I guess like Brandon, he's actually smart.

The bookshelf next. There are two photos in frames. One of two boys—maybe twelve—holding up fish with proud smiles. I recognize Brandon's curly hair and Ryan's blue eyes. They've been friends a long time, I guess. The other is an even younger boy with a man and woman, in front of a Christmas tree. His parents? He said they were killed by a drunk driver. I wonder how old he was. To lose your parents at a young age…

I put the photo back, shoving down my guilt. It was a bad idea to come here. Zoe was right. The more I get to know him, the harder this gets.

I try to harden myself. I've lost my parents before in a lifetime in ancient Egypt. It sucked, but you can get through it.

A book on the shelf catches my eye. A library book, probably way overdue. *Ancient Greek Mythology*. Ding ding ding!

I know I'm pushing my luck. Zoe can't still be talking to Ryan's grandma. I need to get out of here. But I flip through the pages frantically. I land on a section that's been highlighted. The myth of Orion. "Gotcha," I say. This is it. Proof that he knows who he is. Or at least suspects.

Another knock sounds in the background, and I freeze. Another knock? What the hell? I look out the window of Ryan's room and see the tail end of a vehicle. Not Zoe's Volvo. A Deschutes County Sheriff's car.

I hiss and press myself against the wall. *Shit.*

I hear a man's voice from the front door. The name "Deputy Romano." My eyes widen. *Double shit.*

CHAPTER 12

My thoughts are jumbled and panicked, spinning every which way. But there are two that come through strongest.

One: Deputy Romano is here. Two: I need to get the hell out of here—stat.

What happened to Zoe? Was she on the front stoop when the deputy arrived? But no, the deputy knocked on the door. Which meant Zoe had already finished talking to Ryan's grandma. I pray that the deputy didn't see her.

Why is he here? Is Ryan somehow a suspect in the hit-and-run accident that killed my sister? I don't understand how that can be. His truck is still safely parked at Zoe's cabin. I can't think of anything else that would clue them in.

All these thoughts fly through my mind in a blink, but none of it really matters. The only thing that matters right now is getting out of this house.

I stand pressed against the wall of Ryan's room with my ears perked, listening to the muffled conversation in the living room.

I need to go—now. I start to dart into the kitchen and

make a run for it when I hear Ryan's grandmother offer Deputy Romano some tea. I spin and leap back into the bedroom, landing as softly as I can on the thin carpet. My breath is coming in fast bursts. I think I might be hyperventilating. Is this what hyperventilating feels like?

"No, thank you," the deputy says.

I listen to see if Grandma is planning on getting herself something from the kitchen. But it seems that they've settled into the living room. It's now or never.

I run fast and low up towards the kitchen. I can't even look at them as I head through the hallway, from which there's a clear view from the living room. I have this insane thought that if I don't look at them, they won't look at me. It must take fewer than ten seconds, but my bid for freedom feels like an eternity. I close the sliding glass door gingerly and press myself against the side of the house, listening for any sign that my flight has been noticed. Not that I can hear much over the roaring of my pulse in my eardrums.

But no one comes out, not Deputy Romano with this gun drawn or poor Ryan's grandma with a concerned expression. It seems I made a successful escape.

I creep around the side of the house, chewing on my lip.

Zoe's car is nowhere to be found. She must have backed out of the driveway, not wanting to draw suspicion by lingering. Smart girl. I hope she's parked somewhere nearby.

I decide not to run up the driveway, as I think it's visible from the living room. In one quick jolt of speed that would make any four-hundred-meter sprinter proud, I make for the tree line, darting through ferns and bushes into the underbrush. I flatten myself against a tree trunk, peering around to see if there's any movement. The house looks quiet.

I heave a shaky sigh of relief and begin skirting the edge of the trees, making my way back up the driveway to the main road.

Zoe's car is parked on the shoulder, a few hundred yards up the road. I run for it and when I open the door to slide into the passenger side, Zoe lets out a screech, her hand flying onto her chest.

"Mer," she says, "you scared the crap out of me. I thought you were a goner in there."

"Me too," I say, my laughter belying my nervousness. Holy crap, that was close. "Well, that clinches it. I'm officially not cut out to be a spy."

"Right?! I thought I was going to pee my pants up there just asking her if she wanted to donate to the Summit High track team."

"You didn't." I laugh.

"She's so sweet. She donated five bucks!" Zoe says, putting the car into drive and hitting the gas. "I stuck it in her mailbox. Seems like they need it more than us."

I shake my head, amazed we just pulled that off.

"What's that?" Zoe asks, nodding at me. I'd forgotten the book on Greek mythology was still in my hand. "I found it in Ryan's room. The parts on Orion are highlighted." I look at her meaningfully.

She whistles. "Sounds like he has some explaining to do."

"Don't ask him about it until I get back," I say. I still have to go home, and Zoe still has to go back and feed Ryan. "I'll try to come in the morning."

She nods. "You're the boss."

When we arrive at my house I hop out of Zoe's car and pull my bike off the rack. "Thank you, Zoe," I say through her unrolled window.

She gives me a little salute.

I enter through the side door to the garage and drop my bike off. When I come into the living room, both my parents are sitting there at the counter waiting for me, mostly-empty wine glasses in front of them. *Crap.*

"Hi," I say lamely. My dad adjusts his dark-rimmed glasses and looks to my mom with what I imagine is the look that means: 'Should you take this one or will I?' I was in for it.

$$\sim$$

TURNS OUT THEY TOOK TURNS. An hour later, I had been thoroughly lectured by both my parents on the perils of skipping practice, failing to live up to your commitments, and their general disappointment with me as a human being and daughter. I promised never to do it again and professed my undying loyalty to them.

They fed me leftover lasagna and limp salad from one of those prepackaged bags, and by my mom's furrowed brow, I could tell she was thinking about the accident.

"I'm fine," I insist as I put my plate in the dishwasher. Of course this is a lie. I'm so far from fine. But not for the reasons she thinks.

She purses her lips. "Skipping practice isn't like you." Her tone has softened from the drill sergeant persona she adopted earlier. "Neither is being late. We're here to talk about whatever you need."

"I know," I say. "Thanks. Feeling kind of tired, though. I'm gonna call it a night."

"What's this?" she asks, spinning around the book on Greek mythology that I deposited on the countertop. "Bend High School library? Who do you know that goes there?"

"Just a friend of Zoe's," I manage, feeling my web of lies tightening around me. Poor Zoe. I was pulling her deeper and deeper into this mess.

"You doing a project?" my mom asks.

"Could say that," I reply. I put my hand out and she hands the book to me reluctantly. "Night," I say, heading upstairs.

"Night, Dad!" I call. He's been excused from the remainder of the parental lecture and is back in his study.

"Night, jelly bean," he calls to me, my stupid nickname from when I was five. I still kinda like it, though. But only when Dad says it.

Once in my room, I sag against my door, suddenly exhausted. Today has felt like ten days.

I sit on my bed and flip through the mythology book. There's more highlighting on the one page that deals with the Pleiades. There's neat handwriting in the margin and I squint to make it out. It must be Ryan's. I don't know why it matters to me what his handwriting looks like, but I find myself filing away the detail. Another piece of the puzzle that is Ryan Kearney. "What about the seventh? Lost sister?" it reads. He's talking about me. Does it mean he's been looking for me? But why? To kill me, like the others?

I slam the book shut. I'm having such a hard time reconciling the Orion I knew in past lives with this Ryan. He doesn't seem like a murderer, and it unsettles me. It doesn't add up. Electra's death last night was an accident, I believe that. Ryan had a seizure while driving. I mean, he shouldn't have been driving, but I get it. It's hard to give up your freedom, especially when someone depends on you. Were deaths in prior lifetimes accidents, too? I think of him in the alley of Istanbul with his scalpel, his eyes gleaming in the dark. A shiver goes through me. No, they couldn't all have been accidents. There's something corrupt in his soul. Maybe it just hasn't come out yet in this lifetime.

I don't think I'll be able to get a lick of sleep that night, but somehow my eyes grow heavy, and I'm out.

I have a dream. Not a dream—but a vision. Sometimes I'm awake when they come on, but when I'm asleep, I can still tell. My visions have a different quality than regular dreams. The colors are richer, and every sensation is stronger. I can feel the texture of the notebook in my hand, the gentle breeze toying with my hair. I can smell fresh-cut grass and the sweetness of flowers.

I look around, blinking in the sun. I'm in a backyard. A tidy craftsman sits above us surrounded by green lawn, raised boxes filled with tiny shoots of vegetables nestled against its foundation. I pan slowly, trying to get my bearings. The backyard borders a swiftly-moving river—tall trees across the water bow gracefully in the wind.

Then I see Ryan. He turns and looks at me, smiling. I realize I've never seen his smile in real life, but somehow my vision knows. It's devastating—lighting up his whole face. He waves and I hurry towards him. He's standing on the edge of a dock. One hand is in the pocket of his jeans, the other adjusting his sunglasses.

He looks down at something in the water below.

"What is it?" I ask when I reach him.

"Look," he says, putting his free hand on my back. There's a familiarity between us that alarms me, even as it feels right.

I looked down into the cyan water, through the sparkling sunlight.

That's when I see her. Floating. Her blonde hair gently undulating with the lapping of the water.

It's Alcyone. My middle sister.

And she's dead.

CHAPTER 13

I surge into consciousness, gasping for air. Goosebumps pebble my skin; I've broken out in a cold sweat. Watery morning light slants through my blinds. It's just after dawn. My hands shake and I ball them in my comforter to keep them still.

I thought I would have more time. Sometimes years pass between visions—between my sisters' deaths. It's so soon. Electra died just two days ago. I don't know when this vision will come true—it might stay with me for months before she finally dies. But it will come true. They always do.

I scrub my face with my clammy hands, trying to banish the image of her pale skin translucent under the water. This was the warning I needed. The kick in the ass I didn't realize I'd been waiting for. My resolve to do what was necessary had been slipping as I got to know Ryan. Talking to him, learning about his life, seeing photos of his friends, his family. These were things I had never done in my past lifetimes. They were things I shouldn't have done this time.

"Idiot," I hiss at myself, throwing off the covers.

I should have shot him the moment I saw him. My sister

died anyway—calling 911 had done nothing to help her. It had only set this whole mess in motion. Gotten Zoe involved. Made me doubt myself.

I trudge down the hall to the bathroom. I turn on the water and step into the shower, letting the heat scald me and wash away some of the punch of the vision. My mind races as I try to figure out my next move. I need to go over there this morning. I need to end it.

I finish showering and turn off the water, wondering how the hell I'm going to get out of school. Especially with Mom watching me like a hawk after I missed practice yesterday. But I told her I was sick…I can work with that.

I throw on my baggy Summit track sweats and an old T-shirt and head downstairs. Dad's in the kitchen, getting his lunch together. He wears olive khakis and a navy blue quarter-zip sweater. His short brown hair is the same color as mine, his lean, athletic form the same as mine too. I know it's not fair to Mom, and I wouldn't admit it even under threat of torture, but Dad's my favorite. We just…understand each other.

"Morning, jelly bean," he says. "You're up early."

"Dad, I just threw up," I say. "I think I have the flu or something." I pray he buys it. I suck at lying.

His brow furrows and he comes around the island, putting his hand on my forehead. I don't know why parents think the hand on the forehead is some sort of medical crystal ball. But it seems to be their go-to move. "You don't feel warm," he says. "But I suppose missing one day won't hurt. Do you think you can go back to sleep?"

I nod wearily, donning my most pathetic expression.

He ruffles my hair. "I'll tell your mom you're staying home. Rest up and kick this bug."

"Thanks, Dad." I move slowly, shuffling back up the stairs. My heart is racing as I tuck myself back into bed. The truth is, I do feel nauseous. My gut is twisting at the thought of what I'm going to have to do.

A few minutes later, my mom looks into my room. I pretend to be asleep. She clucks her tongue and closes the door. Mom would've pushed me harder to go to school; Dad's more of a softie. But now that he said it was okay for me to stay home, Mom's not going to contradict him. A girl learns a thing or two in her years. When the garage door finally opens and shuts, I spring out of bed like a coiled wire.

I touch the book on my desk briefly, my fingers lingering on the cover. I pull on my jeans, my favorite purple plaid shirt, and my Chuck Taylors. I grab my fleece, zipping it up. I realize in a moment of panic that my bracelet is gone. The only evidence of its absence is the welt where Ryan ripped it off me when we were grappling for the Taser. I feel unsettled without it—unlucky. I banish the thought. I'll have it back within the hour.

Orion and I have been dancing around this showdown for centuries. I just need to get it over with.

The day is overcast and cloudy, with a chill in the air.

As I'm riding over, I call Zoe, cradling my phone awkwardly between my cheek and shoulder.

She picks up quickly. It's still half an hour before school starts.

"Hey. Why are you calling?" She sounds nonplussed.

"Riding my bike. Can't text."

"Ah. Did you get the wrath of Mom yesterday?" she asks.

"You can't imagine."

"I got so many deets on Brandon from Ryan last night," she says, her voice breathless.

I recoil slightly. "How long were you over there?"

"Well, I went back to feed him dinner," she says, "and we talked for, like, an hour maybe? They've been best friends since they were kids. Ryan practically lives over there. He works at their farm. They're as close as brothers." I digest this information. Zoe is clearly beyond excited to get the inside scoop on Brandon Cook. But it doesn't change what I have to do.

I feel a stab of guilt that I'll be killing Zoe's crush's bestie. Maybe she can comfort him in his grief or something.

"Ryan's actually pretty cool—" Zoe says, and I have to stop her before I hear anymore.

"Zoe," I say, interrupting her. "I had another vision last night."

There's silence on the other end of the line.

"Another one of my sisters is going to die."

"Are you sure?" Her voice is small.

"I don't know when, but if I don't do something, it's going to happen. It always happens how the visions show."

"Was it bad?" Zoe asks.

"She drowned." I pause. "I can't let that happen. Not when I can stop it."

"Yeah. I get it." She sounds like the light has been drained from her. "What're you going to?"

"I'm riding over there right now. I'm going to do what I should've done the night Electra died."

"I'm coming," Zoe says. "I'll ditch French. You shouldn't have to do this alone."

"No!" I practically shout at her. I take a breath. "I don't want you anywhere near us. If someone hears the shot or finds out what I did... I won't do that to you, Zoe. Your parents would, like, die."

"I can see the Christmas card now. *Jason's in his third year at MIT, majoring in biomechanical engineering. We have no other child.*"

I manage a halfhearted laugh. "I'll text you when it's done." I hang up before she can protest any further.

It's not just that I want her safely far away, though that's part of it. But that's not all. My friendship with her grounds me in this life. This body, this lifetime. S'mores and track meets and texting under the covers when I should be asleep. With Zoe, I'm Meriah. And today I need to be who I once was. I need to step back into that world of ruthless gods and drama and punishment and tragedy. I need Merope. Daughter of a Titan.

My mouth is dry as I arrive at the cabin. I get off my bike and lean it against the front porch. I take a deep breath and make a desperate attempt to center myself. Quick and painless. I can give him that much. I'll walk into the kitchen, grab the pistol, and end it.

I push through the front door, striding halfway into the living room before I realize what's wrong.

A single word escapes my lips. "Fuck."

The chair is empty, the ropes discarded on the floor.

Ryan is gone.

CHAPTER 14

I'm stunned.

The whole ride here I was psyching myself up to do what needs to be done, and now Ryan is gone. I scream my frustration into the empty room and spin around, pushing back onto the porch.

His truck is still here—he must not have found where we hid the keys. Which means he's on foot. I don't know how long he's been gone, but I have to try to find him. Maybe he only broke free a few minutes ago.

I run into the kitchen and reach under the sink where we hid his keys and his phone. I grab both. At least I know he hasn't called anyone—the cabin doesn't have a landline. Then I open the drawer and retrieve my dad's pistol.

My hands shake as I run out into the yard and get up into his truck.

My mind is racing. If I were Ryan, where I would go? One of the other houses? No. Most of these cabins are summer homes, so they'll be empty. If I were him, I'd go up to the road and try to flag down a car. I squeal out of the driveway and up the dirt road back to the main road.

I drum my fingers on the steering wheel in agitation. My back is as straight as a board as I peer forwards, looking through the trees lining the shoulder of the road. Where is he?

I fear that he left hours ago, and I have no chance of catching him. He could be back to town by now; he could be talking to the police. Giving them my description. Zoe's description.

But they haven't been out to the cabin yet. And he'd have to explain the hit-and-run, so maybe that's not where he's headed. I pray that he thinks it through and decides against involving the authorities. After all, he has to wonder if they'll believe him when he says he didn't leave the scene of the accident on purpose, that he was kidnapped by two high school girls.

I'm peering into the woods on either side of the road, my gaze so intent that I don't see when a figure jumps out into the road a few hundred yards ahead.

He's waving his hands, trying to flag me down. It's Ryan.

I slam on the brakes and skid to a stop. I see his face change from relief to horror when he recognizes the truck and then who's behind the wheel.

Before he has a chance to run, I raise the pistol and point it at him.

His eyes go even wider and he raises his hands.

I throw the truck in park and shoulder open the door, still holding the gun pointed right at him.

"Easy, Louise," he says, his hands still up. "You don't want to do this."

I keep holding the pistol up, gripping it with both hands to keep from shaking.

I jerk my head towards the trees lining the road. "Move."

"I don't want to do that," he says.

"Move!" I scream at him. I can feel myself coming

unhinged. Any moment someone could come by.

He flinches, but he starts into the trees.

My relief is overwhelming. We walk deeper into the underbrush off the road until I can barely see the truck through the trees. "Stop," I say.

He's shaking his head at me as he turns to face me. "You're going to kill me?" he asks, disbelieving. "You're seriously going to kill me. What the hell is wrong with you? Who are you? What the hell did I ever do to you?"

My chest tightens as I see their faces flash before my eyes. I shove the memories down, trying to hold back tears. *Oh, god*, I think. *I will do this without crying.*

"At least tell me why. If I'm going to die, at least do me the favor of being honest with me. You owe me that much," he says. I know he's stalling, and I know I should kill him, but part of me wants to tell him. Part of me is desperately curious how much he knows. His notes in the book, my name on his lips as his body convulsed. I have to know. I'm a movie villain falling into the oldest trap in the book. But I can't help myself.

"You want to know?" I say.

"*Yes.*" His answer is angry.

I don't blame him. "My name isn't Louise."

"Yeah, I figured that," he says sarcastically.

I huff. "Do you want to hear or not?"

He gives me a single nod.

"My name is Meriah," I tell him. "But that's only my name in this lifetime. My real name is—"

"Merope," he finishes. His eyes go wide, his face white. He goes to reach in his pocket and I stiffen. "Hey! Stop!"

"Easy," he says. "I have your bracelet." He pulls it out, letting it dangle from his fingers. "The Pleiades. I know this constellation. You're one of them, aren't you?"

Zeus's balls. He actually knows me. I nod. "I'm the reincarnated version of Merope—a nymph from Ancient Greece. And you are the reincarnated version of—"

"Orion. I'm the reincarnated version of Orion. I know you," he says. "I mean… I-I did."

I lick my lips. "How do you know? You've never known before. Have you?"

"I don't think so. But when I have a seizure, I see things. I thought I was going crazy at first when I was young…but they were so real. Like past lifetimes. Different faces, different forms. I didn't understand how my brain could be that creative."

I realize the gun is lowered and I raise it back up.

"If you know who you are, then you know why you have to die. You've killed my sisters hundreds of times. You're a murder, and it's starting again. You killed Electra two nights ago."

"I didn't mean to," Ryan says, pleading with me. "It was an accident."

"It doesn't matter," I say. "The fact is they're innocent and you're not. You have to die."

I'm shaking now—unwelcome tears stinging my eyes. I've never in all my lifetimes been able to talk to someone about this. Someone who was there, who understands the disjointed feeling of having a hundred lifetimes in your head. I've never been able to talk to anyone, and now I have to kill the only person who understands. The injustice of it takes my breath away. I told you the Fates are bitches.

"Don't do this," Ryan says quietly. "It's not my fault. Zeus —he did this."

"It doesn't matter," I say again, trying to convince myself as much as him. "It doesn't matter if he wields the weapon— you are the blade. And I'm not going to let you cut down any more of my sisters." I cock the gun.

"What the fuck is going on?" a new voice says.

CHAPTER 15

*W*hat is going on indeed?

My heart painfully squeezes in my chest as I recognize the owner of the new voice. It's Brandon Cook. Why is Brandon Cook standing in the middle of the forest, ruining the hardest thing I'll ever have to do?

Brandon doesn't seem to realize what he's done. He's wearing jeans, old school Pumas, and his green and black letter jacket. "Why is Meriah Carmichael pointing a gun at you?" Brandon asks. He's looking back and forth between us like he cannot make heads or tails of what's going on.

"It's complicated," Ryan says weakly.

I lower the gun, fighting a wave of tears that threatens to overwhelm me. I can't kill Ryan in front of Brandon. Not without getting rid of the witness. And that's out of the question. Brandon is innocent in all this. There's no way I'd kill him too. Not to mention Zoe would *never* forgive me.

"Meriah," Ryan says slowly and carefully, like I'm a wild animal that might lash out at any moment. He raises a hand slowly. His fingers shake. "Give me the gun."

"Not a chance," I retort. A little thrill goes through me at hearing my name on his lips and I hate myself for it.

Brandon steps forwards, bold but calm. "Will you give me the gun?" I see why Zoe likes him. Even if he wasn't so distractingly cute with those easy curls and bright blue eyes, he has a way about him that's magnetic. It makes you want to trust him. It makes you want him to trust you. To like you. "Whatever the hell is going on between you two," Brandon continues, "we can all agree that I'm not going to kill anyone."

I heave a sigh and uncock the weapon, resigned. I hand it to him, handle first.

Ryan hisses out a breath of relief as the weapon passes from my fingers, sinking down into a crouch, his head in his hands.

"Now who's going to tell me what's going on?"

"It's complicated," I say, echoing Ryan. I don't know what happens now. I should be worried about convincing Ryan not to press charges against me for kidnapping and attempted murder, but all I can see is my sister's pale face floating beneath the water. I guess I failed in this lifetime, too. I shouldn't be so surprised.

Ryan surges back to his feet, his hands in his hair, turning it wild. "Can we just talk?" Ryan asks. "Please. I feel like we need to talk."

I shake my head. "Fine."

The three of us trudge back to the road and I see Brandon's maroon Pathfinder behind Ryan's truck. "How did you find us?" I ask.

"I hadn't heard from Ryan in a few days, so I used the find-my-iPhone function," he replies.

"How? I thought you could only do that with your own phone."

"Ryan's on my family's phone plan," Brandon says, shooting a look towards Ryan that seems almost apologetic.

"But we turned it off," I say lamely. Silently, I curse myself. Betrayed by the phone. Frickin' technology. I might as well have posted a pic with a tied-up Ryan on my Instagram feed. #Kidnappersofinstagram!

"It registers the last place the phone was," Brandon explains.

"I'm riding with Brandon," I say. The thought of being alone with an untied Ryan in the cab of his truck sets my nerves on edge. "Let's go back to the cabin. We can talk there."

Ryan nods. "Don't really ever want to see the place again. But okay."

"What cabin?" Brandon asked, but I'm already headed towards the car.

I get into Brandon's Pathfinder. It has a black leather interior and smells clean—like someone just detailed it. A little baseball hangs from the rearview mirror. It's a far cry from Ryan's truck. Zoe told me about them being friends, as close as brothers. I ponder the revelation that Ryan is on Brandon's family's phone plan. I guess he's really become a part of their family.

"So," Brandon says, chewing on his plush bottom lip as he throws the car into reverse. "Finish your history essay yet?"

I let out a strangled laugh. "You must think I'm a complete psychopath." I groan, dropping my head into my hands.

"I mean, it's not looking great for you," he says, "but I'm willing to be convinced."

"Believe me when I say I don't want to kill Ryan," I say. The truth of it hits me like a slap in the face. I've learned a few things in the last forty-eight hours. First, I'm not a killer

—the thought of ending anyone is enough to tie me up in knots. But two, the more disturbing realization, is that I would specifically never kill Ryan Kearney. I would miss his stupid perfect face.

I groan. "What a nightmare," I mutter to myself. I *am* a psychopath. Because only a psychopath has a crush on a murderer.

"It'll be okay, Meriah," Brandon says. And when he says it, I almost believe him.

"You skipped history to come find Ryan?"

He nods. "Dude doesn't just not show up for work or not respond to texts for two days. He's as reliable as clockwork. At first I thought maybe he was mad at me or needed some space for some reason, but then I talked to his Gran and she said she hadn't seen him either…"

I direct Brandon down the lane to Zoe's cabin and we pull into the driveway and get out. Ryan parks behind us and we all trudge inside.

Brandon's eyebrows raise as he sees the chair with the ropes.

My face heats.

"Kinky," is all he says.

Ryan shakes his head.

"I'm hungry," Brandon says. "There anything to eat up in this joint?"

Teenage boys. They're like velociraptors when it comes to food. "There might still be some pizza in the fridge," I say. I couldn't eat if my life depended on it. My stomach feels like it just got the wrong end of a roller coaster ride.

Ryan and I stare at each other in silence as Brandon heads to the kitchen and rifles around. Ryan looks exhausted, dark shadows smudging the skin beneath his deep blue eyes. A pang of guilt strikes me as I realize what I put him through. I do my best to squash it, but my effort is weak. I'm too tired to run from my feelings anymore. I pull his phone out of my back pocket and hand to him. "I guess you'll need this back."

"Now that I'm not dead," he says angrily.

I look away. "I guess I deserve that."

"You killed me before?" he asks. "In other lifetimes? I don't remember."

I shake my head. "No, I've never tried it before. It was a… new theory."

"Can't say I'm fond of it."

"I'm sick of doing nothing," I snap. "Sick of feeling useless. I can't just let them keep dying."

Ryan opens his mouth to reply, but Brandon interrupts, calling from the kitchen. "Dude, there's hot chocolate in here! And marshmallows! You guys want any?"

I look at Ryan with a puzzled expression. He shrugs. "Brandon has the rare ability to be comfortable in any situation."

I think about it. Hot chocolate suddenly sounds amazing. Something to do with my shaking hands. Something to focus on besides Ryan's piercing gaze. "Yes, please," I holler.

"Bro?" Brandon asks.

"Sure," Ryan says, rolling his eyes.

We're both still standing awkwardly, facing off against each other. I turn the chair around towards the couch and sit gingerly. The thing isn't very comfortable.

"Try sleeping in it," Ryan says, as if he can read my thoughts.

I look away, anywhere but at him. When I look at him I can't stop myself from examining his every feature. Even unshowered, in three-day-old clothes, he is handsome, his mussed hair making him look like he's just woken up from a nap, like I've intruded upon some private scene I have no right to see. I find myself thinking about what the muscles of his chest and arms must look like underneath his flannel. I'm hyperaware of his movements, how he rubs together the calluses on the tips of his fingers, how one of his booted feet taps the ground as he waits.

Just when I think I might scream to break the silence between us, Brandon emerges from the kitchen bearing two steaming mugs of hot chocolate.

"Here you go, princess," Brandon says with mock sweetness as he hands one to Ryan. "Extra marshmallows."

"Thanks, Mom," Ryan replies, batting his sweeping eyelashes.

I take mine. "Thanks." Their banter reminds me of mine and Zoe's. A new wave of guilt crashes over me as I think that I almost just robbed Brandon of his closest friend. I don't admire him the way that Zoe does, but he always seemed like a nice guy. He doesn't deserve to have his best friend die. But my sisters don't deserve to die either. The fact is, I don't want anyone to die. It's this damn curse.

Brandon comes back with two pieces of pizza and another mug of hot chocolate.

"Talk about breakfast of champions," I comment.

He nods. "So this has been the hideout?" He takes it in. "Is your place?"

"No," I say. "It belongs to my friend Zoe. You know her?"

Brandon nods. "Junior class president? Cute Asian chick?"

I file that away. *So he thinks she's cute*, I think. That'll keep Zoe going for years.

Brandon looks between us. "So who's going to go first? I'm in the mood for a good story."

I take a deep breath. I don't know how to start. It'll sound insane. I gather my courage, fortifying myself with a sip of hot chocolate. The marshmallows have mostly dissolved, leaving a layer sugary foam on the top. I open my mouth to begin speaking when Zoe bursts through the front door.

"Mer!" she yells before freezing in her tracks. She takes in Ryan and Brandon sitting on the couch—takes in me in the chair. Takes in the mugs of hot chocolate and the half-eaten piece of pizza in Brandon's hand.

"What'd I miss?" she asks, offering a weak smile.

Zoe is placated by a mug of hot chocolate made and delivered by Brandon Cook. The guys scoot over on the sofa to make room for her, and I can tell from the gleam in her eye that whatever madness I've put her through has now been deemed totally, completely worth it.

Ryan and I look at each other, both tongue-tied, each daring the other to start.

Brandon interrupts our standoff as the voice of reason. I see why Ryan likes this guy. "Meriah, as the party who was holding the deadly weapon, why don't you explain first?"

I close my eyes, steeling myself. "It's going to sound fantastical," I say. "I need you to suspend disbelief for a while."

I plunge forwards before I lose my nerve. "I'm the reincarnated version of an ancient Greek nymph-Titan. Ryan is the reincarnation of an Ancient Greek hunter who worked for Zeus. Zeus was really pissed at my sisters 'cause they tried to steal this ancient weapon, so he cursed my sisters by having Ryan murder them every lifetime." Oh, god. Brandon's going to think I need to be seriously medicated. I soldier on. "I'm a seer, and I see the future. I saw that Ryan was going to murder another one of my sisters, and so I decided to kill him to prevent it." I close my eyes.

Brandon glances at Ryan.

"You're a seer?" Ryan asks, as if that explains everything. "Is that why you were there the night of the accident?"

I nod grimly.

"What accident?" Brandon asks Ryan. "Are you saying you believe all that?"

He sighs. "The basics are right. Though I don't like the insinuation that I *murdered* your sisters." He emphasizes the word. "I never murdered anyone."

I scoff. "Tell that to my sisters."

"Murder implies intent. I never *meant* to kill anyone."

"Bullshit," I say, my face heating. How dare he deny what he's done? Rationalize it away? "What about Istanbul?" I practically spit at him. "I saw you there that night in the alley. Carving her chest open. I saw her blood on your hands…you were a butcher!" A lump grows in my throat as the memory floods over me.

"Istanbul?" Ryan is incredulous. "I was a surgeon in that lifetime! I found her dying in that alley after being stabbed and attacked by someone else! I was trying to save her life!"

I recoil, searching my memory. Could that be true? Could I have misinterpreted what I saw that night?

"Yes, Merope and her sisters were cursed," Ryan says. "But I was cursed more than all of you! Lifetime after lifetime, the Fates would take them, no matter how I tried to prevent their deaths. I was a surgeon, I was a soldier, I was the infected guy who didn't realize it until everyone else was coughing and it was too late. The Fates are infinitely creative in finding ways to kill. Do you know what it's like to accidentally kill someone? To have the weight of their death on your conscience?"

"It can't be much worse than watching them die and not being able to stop it," I say woodenly, unable to process what he's telling me. That he doesn't want to kill them.

"Who's Merope?" Brandon asks.

Zoe laughs. "It's her former life. Her first Greek identity. He's Orion."

"Like the constellation?"

Ryan nods.

Brandon blows out a breath. "I think this hot chocolate was past its sell-by date. Because you're all taking crazy. You believe this, Zoe?"

"Yes," Zoe says. "Mer and I have been friends a long time. I was there when she first started seeing the visions. Remembering her past lives. The stuff she told me... A twelve-year-old couldn't make it up. She wouldn't have. It was scary as hell."

Brandon's eyes go wide and he looks at Ryan. "The seizures?"

Ryan nods, taking a sip.

"You should have told me, man," Brandon says gently. "You could have told me."

"I didn't want you to think I was crazy." Ryan examines the dregs of his mug. "Your family...I didn't want to lose you guys."

"You wouldn't have."

Ryan's Adam's apple bobs as he nods his thanks.

"So you believe them?" Zoe asks Brandon.

"I guess. Better than the alternative."

"Which is...?" Zoe asks.

"Thinking that my best friend, the girl who sits next to me in history, and the junior class president are all totally loco."

We all let out a nervous chuckle at that. "Do you see the future too?" I ask Ryan. "In your visions? Or just the past?"

"Past only," he says. I'm not sure why, but I'm relieved. I guess I've just gotten used to being the only one with the ability to see the future.

"So you two have never talked about this before?" Brandon points between me and Ryan. "Even in…past lifetimes?"

I shake my head. "We've always been enemies. I focused on trying to stop him from killing my sisters. But I've always failed. Zeus's curse is too strong."

Ryan's lips curl down. Even with a frown etched across his features, he's handsome as hell. Could it be possible, what he says? That he's not the villain in all this? That he's as much a victim as any of us? "I wouldn't call it a curse."

"I didn't know we were debating semantics." I bristle. "What would *you* call it when an all-powerful deity casts a spell requiring you to be reborn and die lifetime after lifetime?"

"Zeus doesn't give two shits about you all. Or me, for that matter. He just wanted the scythe back. He didn't cast any spell. It was an accident."

I still. My limbs go cold. "What do you mean?"

"The scythe backfired…you really don't remember?"

I shake my head.

"What scythe?" Zoe asks.

"What the hell is a scythe?" Brandon echoes.

I let out a little laugh. I haven't told Zoe all the details of how the curse came to be. I'm not sure why I kept this piece from her. Maybe because I don't like going back to that day. It's too painful to relive our foolishness. Our folly in thinking we could pull one over on Zeus when even our dad, one of the most powerful Titans in the world, couldn't defeat him.

"A scythe is like a sharp curved knife pole thingy that you use to cut grain. But this one wasn't like that. It was a weapon owned by Chronos, the Titan who ruled the world before Zeus. He was god of time," I explain.

"Naturally," Brandon says. His cheeks are pink. I get the feeling that he's about to head back into the kitchen for a bowl of popcorn.

"Merope…Meriah, and her sisters were trying to steal the scythe," Ryan adds, his tone a little judgy for my taste. "Zeus didn't want them to. I went with him to help him stop them."

"Ryan shot me with an arrow," I counter, "and I blacked out. So I don't remember what happened next."

"You shot her?" Brandon says. "Dick move, bro."

I feel vindicated. That's right—Orion *did* shoot me. *That* was no accident. So maybe all of this "it was all accidental, I'm not a murderer" business is a load of crap.

Ryan huffs. "It was a different time then. I was working for Zeus, and they were stealing his property! Anyway, it's not important. I guess Mer did pass out. But her sisters wouldn't give up the scythe without a fight."

"Hold up. How many sisters?" Brandon asks.

"Six," Zoe, Ryan, and I all reply. I try to ignore the fact that Ryan called me "Mer" and I kind of liked it.

"Nice," Brandon says appreciatively, as if we're talking about how many Playboy Bunnies were at the mansion. "Okay, continue."

"Atlas's daughters were not without skills. They fought me and Zeus—it was madness in close quarters. Maia, Mer's oldest sister, had the scythe, and she swung it at Zeus's head. He held up a hand to block it and caught it. In that moment, it was like time stopped. Zeus and Maia were both trying to wrench the scythe out of each other's hands. I'm not exactly sure what happened, but I think Zeus sent a lightning bolt through the scythe to try to fry Maia and make her let go."

"Douchebag," I mutter.

"It backfired. Everything went white. I didn't come to

until my next life. That's when I began to realize that some-thing was wrong. That something had happened."

My mind was reeling. After more than two thousand years, Ryan had just filled in a piece of the puzzle. But did I believe him? That Zeus hadn't done it on purpose? That my sisters and Orion's bodies splashed across the night sky, their souls reborn again and again…That it was all…a cosmic accident?

"Are you guys thinking what I'm thinking?" Brandon asks.

"That this would make a seriously good Netflix show?" Zoe offers.

"Obvi, yes," Brandon agrees. "But not just that. If Zeus didn't curse you guys on purpose, why don't you just go ask him to undo it? To use this scythe thingy and erase it all?"

My mouth falls open as the force of Brandon's suggestion bowls into me like a gale-force wind. The future opens up before me, a potential where I'm not beset by visions of the past or the future. Where I'm just a regular girl with a regular life. My eyes trace Ryan's features of their own volition. With a regular boyfriend.

A new purpose flares within me, as bright and powerful as a firework. We're going to break the curse.

CHAPTER 17

Ryan's cold voice of reason smothers my excitement like a wet blanket. "It sounds great. But does anyone actually know how to find an ancient Greek god? It's not like we can just traipse over to Greece and knock on the door of Mount Olympus. Does anyone even have a passport?"

Brandon, Zoe, and I nod.

Ryan scowls.

Brandon has the wherewithal to look apologetic. "You know we went to Cabo a few years back."

"My parents like to ski in Whistler," I offer.

Zoe chimes in. "Yeah, we went to Europe last summer."

"Okay, so I'm the only asshole without a passport. Great." Ryan throws up his hands.

"No, Ryan's right," I say, not sure why I'm trying to make him feel better. "I couldn't exactly explain to my parents why I need to go over there."

"Senior project?" Zoe offers with a weak grin, and Brandon laughs. Her ears turn a pretty shade of pink.

"And there's the issue of money," I continue. "Plane tickets are expensive."

"I think we're getting ahead of ourselves," Brandon says. "Isn't this the part in the movie where there'd be a research montage? Like all of us poring over old, dusty books in some ancient library? We need to figure out (a) where Zeus is now, (b) where the scythe thing is, and (c) how to get him to help us."

"Us?" Ryan asks. "Brandon, I appreciate it, man, but this isn't your fight."

"If it's yours, it's mine. Plus, this is about ten times more interesting than anything else I've got going on."

"Agreed," Zoe says sweetly. "We'll help you guys figure this out."

I smile at Zoe, even though I know that she was totally behind me already, and she would literally be happy picking up dog poop at the park if it meant she got to hang with Brandon.

"So, research," I say. "Our new mission, if we choose to accept it, is to figure out where Zeus and the scythe are now. We could head to the library?"

Brandon wrinkles his nose. "Ew. I was being figurative. Let's just go to a coffee shop and all bring our laptops."

"I hate to be the practical, studious one of our little Scooby gang, but shouldn't we, you know, go to school?" Zoe pulls her phone out. "We can make third period if we leave now."

Oh yeah. School. Crap.

Ryan groans. "God, I don't want to know how much trouble I'm in with Gran. And my teachers. And I missed work..." He tips forwards and buries his face in his hand.

"Don't worry about work," Brandon says. "I'll work it out with Dad. And your gran will understand."

"Um..." I say, not sure how to break this to him.

"What?" He looks up at me, his blue eyes suspicious.

"There may have been a sheriff's deputy at your house when I dropped off the medication for your grandma," I say. "I'm assuming he was looking into your disappearance. He's the same guy who's investigating the hit-and-run."

"The hit-and-run?" Brandon asks.

Ryan surges to his feet, storming across the room, his hands in his hair. Barely restrained energy crackles from him, and for a moment I shy away.

I close my eyes briefly and explain to Brandon the circumstances of Ryan's and my first encounter. He swears.

Ryan turns and shoves through the screen door, headed outside.

I bounce to my feet, alarmed. "Where's he going?"

We all run out after him and find him standing in the driveway, looking at the front of his truck.

The damage isn't too bad, actually. The fender is dented and the right headlight is broken, but the truck is built like a tank. There's no damage to the body at all.

"We can fix that," Brandon says. "Before anyone sees."

Ryan is shaking his head. "No. I need to turn myself in."

Zoe, Brandon, and I all protest in tandem.

"And tell them what?" I ask.

"The truth."

"That you were kidnapped by two teenage girls and held hostage to end an ancient curse?" I ask.

"Well, part of the truth," he amends.

Zoe and I exchange a look of sheer panic. He cannot tell the authorities that we kidnapped him. Life: over. It's one thing if I ruined my own life with this crazy scheme, but not Zoe's. I won't let that happen to her.

I move to stand in front of him, forcing him to look from the truck to me. "Please, Ryan, don't do this. It'll ruin all of our lives."

"No less than we deserve," he says morosely, refusing to meet my eyes. "Don't you think it's time we face the consequences for all this?"

"You and me, maybe, but not Zoe. I brought her into this. She's totally innocent. Don't make her an accessory to a kidnapping. Even if she avoids jail time, she'll never get into college. Please. Don't ruin my best friend's life."

Ryan glances at Zoe, his resolve wavering.

"And what about your life, man?" Brandon asks. "It was an accident. Coming forwards won't do anything but ruin your future."

"It'll give the family closure," Ryan protests. "I haven't always owned up to what I've done…in past lives. I'm tired of being a coward."

"Now is not the time to grow a conscience," Brandon says.

"If you're in jail, how will we break the curse? Find Zeus? More of my sisters will die," I point out.

"Maybe if I'm in jail, they'll be safe from me," he shoots back.

"You know that's not how it works," I say softly.

"What if you wait?" Zoe offers quietly. "Break the curse. Then if you still want to turn yourself in, go ahead."

"Zo, no—" I begin.

"It's okay, Mer. Ryan's right. It's not fair to the family. We'll just tell the police we were messing around. I don't know. We'll figure out something. We're young. We'll just have something extra interesting to write for our college entrance essays."

A bark of laughter escapes me.

"Besides, Ryan wouldn't press charges against us, would he?"

She turns to Ryan, and when I look back, I'm startled to find him looking at me with an intensity that makes me take a step back. He's so hard to read. He has the right to be furious at us for what we did to him. And now, he's free. If he's spiteful, he could make our lives very, very unpleasant. But…I don't think that's who he is.

After a pause, he nods. "Okay. I won't turn myself in until we break the curse. And no, I won't press charges."

I blow out a slow, shaky breath. Thank god.

"We'll have to come up with a good cover story for where you've been," Brandon says, chewing on his lip again. "We can pound out the fender tonight in the shop and I'll pick up a new headlight on the way home."

"Anyone got any bright ideas for a cover story?" Ryan lets out a harsh laugh.

"Ooh!" Brandon says. "You could say you two were shacked up here at Zoe's cabin." He waggles an eyebrow. "So wrapped up in each other that you lost track of time."

"For two days?" Ryan scoffs as I shake my head.

"No. No, no." I wave my hands. I can feel my face heating at the thought of being "shacked up" with Ryan for forty-eight hours. The butterflies in my stomach are trying to tell me that it's not such a bad idea, but I squash them ruthlessly.

"It's not terrible," Zoe says. Traitor. She'd agree with anything Brandon says. "Just say you were watching movie marathons or something. It explains why the cabin has been used, and why both of you guys have been missing school and practice."

"No," Ryan and I say in unison, and we exchange a look, surprised at our sudden alliance.

"I'll think of something," Ryan mutters.

"We should get going," Zoe says, nodding towards her car.

And suddenly the weirdest morning of my life is ending. I can't account for the hesitation I have in leaving the cabin. In going back to normal life. But it's not normal, is it? Everything has changed. I have a new purpose. And new allies.

"Ryan," I call, pausing before I get into the car. The memory of last night's dream has flashed in my mind. My sister floating, dead, the soft strands of her hair drifting in gentle waves.

He looks my way.

"Stay away from the water."

CHAPTER 18

*I*t's Friday night.

Why didn't I realize that it's Friday night? Suddenly, a coffee shop research sesh feels a lot more like a double date.

I stand in my closet amid a pile of clothes. I've tried on and discarded nearly everything I own, but I've settled on jeans, my Chucks, and my "Otter Space" TeeTurtle shirt. Yes, it features adorable otters in space. I'm unsatisfied with the ensemble, but it was the least objectionable of my options. I thread my hair into a loose braid and contemplate putting on makeup. But Ryan has seen me totally casual, so makeup would look more than a little conspicuous.

I throw myself onto my bed, screaming into my pillow.

Part of me wishes Dad had said *no* to me going out tonight, on account of me being sick. But Dad, god love him, can't say *no*. Not when I ask with the big eyes.

I roll over and take a breath, blowing it out slowly. The way my stomach is twisting, I'm starting to think I've actually made myself sick.

I grab my phone and stare at the screen, at the two new contacts listed there. Ryan Kearney. Brandon Cook. Zoe got their numbers at school and texted them to me. My finger itches to text Ryan, but I don't know what I'd say. *Sorry about the kidnapping? Sorry for making you a hit-and-run suspect?* Besides, that would be weird. I'm going to see him in less than an hour.

I keep trying to take stock of what's happened in the last two days, and it keeps slipping from my mental fingers. It feels too big to wrap my brain around. After two millennia, I finally know how my sisters were cursed. I can't decide if it's better or worse that it was all a big misunderstanding. That the curse was an accident, rather than something Zeus did purposely to punish us. Worse. I think it's worse. Though now we do have a sliver of a chance to get him to unravel it.

Zeus was not known for his leniency or his magnanimity. I can't imagine two thousand years have softened him much. He terrified me when I was Merope—though I would have denied it to the grave. But now? I'm a sixteen-year-old mortal from Oregon. The thought of standing before him and asking him for anything…it makes me want to curl under the covers.

But he was always fond of Orion. Orion was a loyal ally to him. Maybe if Ryan does the asking, I can just hang back. Cower in the corner of his throne room or whatever.

I pull my pillow over my face to hide my mortification. I feel so completely obvious. I can't even think about Ryan without blushing. God damn it. I can just imagine what I'd tell our kids. *Well, honey, somewhere between dragging your father's unconscious body out of a truck and Tasing him, I just knew…* I scream into my pillow again. What's wrong with me? Is this some sort of messed-up reverse Stockholm Syndrome?

I try to think objectively—as if I had just met Ryan at school or through track or something. He checks a lot of boxes. Dangerously cute? Check. Not a douchebag? Check. Sporty? Check. Intelligent? Yeah, seems like it. Something about him that makes my skin feel like it's on fire when I'm near him? Check, check. But I know that it's more than that. It's the relief I feel to have finally found someone who understands what I've been through. All of it. The strange double vision of past lives, the twisted memories of girls' deaths. I file through my visions, testing them against his insistence that he never killed on purpose. That it was always an accident. It holds up. It's like my visions have been shifted through a different lens, and suddenly I see the ways that I misinterpreted…that I assumed his ill intent when I didn't know all the facts. How I spent all these years hating and demonizing him…when he was just as broken and hurting as me. I think maybe I owe him a big fat apology.

"Mer!" my dad calls up the stairs. "Zoe's here!"

I pop up, feeling like a bottle rocket about to blow. I grab the book I stole from Ryan and walk down the stairs, doing my best to school my features into nonchalance. I told Dad that Zoe and I are going to meet some other kids to work on a group project. It's half true, anyway.

"You're sure you're feeling up to this?" Dad asks, brushing back my hair as I pass.

I smile weakly. "I'm feeling a lot better. And if I don't go, I'll get assigned all the crappy work."

Dad snorts in sympathy. "Group projects are the worst. Home by nine?"

"Nine?" I ask in dismay.

"You need your rest to kick whatever bug you're fighting. Non-negotiable."

"Okay," I agree.

In the car, Zoe looks like she just won the lottery.

I grin despite myself. "Tone down the glowing, okay?"

"I can't help it!" she squeals. "Brandon talked to me three times at school today! That's three times the amount he talked to me last month."

"I'm glad my curse has been good for your dating life," I say wryly, drumming my fingers nervously on the cover of the book on my lap.

"Oh, it so has." She's dead serious.

"I guess it's my best friend duty to tell you that Brandon said you were cute."

I think you can hear her squeal in the next county.

We pull into the parking lot at Backporch Coffee Roasters, one of our favorite coffee shops. The drive was far too short for my taste. I planned to center myself, to find my zen, but I feel as jittery as a grasshopper. No coffee for me.

Ryan and Brandon are visible through the front window, sitting there at a table. Zoe and I both take a deep breath.

Ryan's old truck hulks over Brandon's SUV in the parking lot. I glance back on the way in, scoping out the front for any sign of the accident. There's nothing except a bit of warping where they must have pounded the dent out of the fender. You wouldn't even see it unless you knew to look. A surge of relief wells in me. There's nothing linking Ryan—and me—to the hit-and-run.

The bell tinkles as we enter the shop. We exchange a round of "heys" as Zoe and I slide into chairs opposite the guys.

Brandon wears his uniform from baseball practice, his curls wild. Ryan is freshly showered and wearing a clean flannel shirt in shades of blue. His hair is slicked back in the spiked, gravity-defying style I saw the first day I kidnapped him, a look that manages to come off as effortless, though I'm sure it takes some doing.

"You guys need coffee?" Brandon asks.

I shake my head.

"I'm gonna grab a latte," Zoe says, starting to stand.

"I'll get it," Brandon says, beating her to his feet. "My treat."

The excitement radiates from Zoe as they go up to order. It leaves Ryan and me, facing off against each other.

I take off my fleece, suddenly feeling like it's about a thousand degrees in here.

"Cool shirt," Ryan says, and I warm to fire-of-a-thousand-suns hot at the compliment. Good wardrobe choice confirmed.

I look down at my space otters. "Thanks."

Silence.

"Everything okay with your grandma?" I ask softly, searching for the best way to wade into the waters of our new uneasy alliance. I spin the bracelet on my wrist, glad I have it back.

Ryan nods. "She was worried sick. But…yeah. I told her I needed some time to myself, so I went camping."

"That happen often?"

"No. I don't think she believed me. But I think she's worried the truth will be worse."

"Ignorance is bliss."

There's awkward silence as Ryan nods again. "Um, here you go." I slide the book across the table.

He spins it around. "Where'd you get this?"

I lick my lips. "When I went to drop off your grandma's medication, I may have…done a little investigating."

His blue eyes widen. "You went in my house? In my room?"

Brandon and Zoe return just in time to hear that and take in the tension between us.

"I'm really sorry. I was still trying to get a read on you. When you had your seizure, I thought you had said my name, but I couldn't be sure. I just wanted to see if there were any clues about who you were."

"And what'd you figure out?" Ryan asks. His tone is gentler but still carries a thread of hostility. He's disconcerted that I was in his space. I get it.

Brandon chimes in, grabbing Ryan's shoulders playfully and giving him a little shake. "That my man needs to do laundry more often, I bet."

"I barely had a minute. I just saw the book, grabbed it, and ran," I say, offering a smile. "I didn't even have time to go through your underwear drawer."

The corner of Ryan's mouth quirks up at that.

"Listen," Zoe says. "Let's forget everything that happened before, okay? We know now that we're all on the same side. That's the most important thing, right?"

"Agreed," I say, my eyes searching Ryan's face.

"Okay," Ryan says.

Brandon retrieves a sleek iBook out of his backpack and pops it open. "Is it time to nerd out?"

"Music to my ears," Zoe says, pulling her laptop out too.

I follow suit.

"I've just got my phone," Ryan says, and I remember the ancient yellowed machine in his room. I feel bad suddenly, like we're all flaunting our easy middle-class status like a bunch of assholes.

"Where do we start?" Brandon asks.

"I guess we look for any signs of Zeus being alive. Or any of the other gods." I jab the power button on my HP. "Miracles, strange occurrences around his temples…" I trail off. How does a person find a god?

"He might still have followers," Ryan adds. "Like a religion or cult. If we find them, they might be able to help us find him."

"Okay, so just deep dive into the world of the internet crazies," Brandon says.

"Pretty much!" Zoe adds.

The hours tick by in a blink. As the sky darkens outside, it grows more comfortable around our table. We all find some seriously weird shit, some of which makes us laugh, some of which makes us wrinkle our noses. Conspiracy theories, strange sightings—there's plenty of craziness to be found, but it feels impossible to tell fact from fiction. None of it gets us closer to finding Zeus or the scythe.

Finally, I slam my laptop shut, rubbing my face. I need to be home in fifteen minutes.

Ryan has long since put his phone away and is now idly spinning the Greek history book on the table before him. Frustration comes off him in waves.

I put my hand out and stop the book from spinning. Our fingers touch, and I feel a spark of connection. "We'll find him," I say, meeting his eyes. I try not to think about the fact that I've already had another vision. We don't have a lot of time.

He pulls his hand back, looking out the window. "I shouldn't have gotten my hopes up."

"It's only day one," Brandon offers.

"But we have no idea where to look," Ryan counters.

I look at the book, at the spot where Ryan's and my fingers met. The book is turned over. The back cover has the picture of the author, a smiling woman in large glasses posed before a bookshelf of tomes. I see her name, and my eyes widen.

I pull the book towards me, skimming her bio eagerly. A jolt of excitement shoots through me.

My head snaps up. "I have an idea."

But they aren't paying attention. They're looking out the

window at the Deschutes County Sheriff's vehicle that just pulled up. And the man who's getting out of it.

"Isn't that…?" Zoe trails off.

"Deputy Romano," I confirm. The name comes out like a curse.

CHAPTER 19

I'm frozen to my seat as the cheerful bell tinkles and Deputy Romano pushes in.

"It could be a coincidence," Zoe hisses, but he's approaching our table. We'll have no such luck.

"Ryan Kearney?" The deputy looks up from his little pad of paper. He must have a photo or something, because his eyes are pinned on Ryan. So much so that he doesn't even look at me. I pray to all that is holy and a few things that aren't so holy that he doesn't notice me. How would I be able to explain that Ryan and I know each other? That I was on scene at the hit-and-run and Ryan disappeared for a few days…long enough to make his grandmother report him missing…

"Yes, sir," Ryan replies. His voice is strong, without a quaver. Guy must have balls of steel. My face heats as I realize that I have no right to be thinking anything about Ryan's balls.

"You mind coming with me to the station? I have a few questions to ask you about the past few days."

"Am I under arrest, sir?" Ryan asks.

"No." Deputy Romano frowns at him. "But you gave your grandmother enough of a scare that she filed a missing person's report. Just need to tie up a few loose ends."

I breathe out a shaky sigh as Zoe's hand finds mine under the table, her fingers twining into mine in a death grip.

Ryan's blue eyes are fixed on the deputy. "If it's all the same, sir, if I'm not under arrest, I'd rather not go down to the station. I'll answer your questions here."

My eyes widen, meeting Brandon's across the table. I revise my assessment about Ryan's balls of steel. The guy has balls of titanium.

Deputy Romano is silent for a moment, his jaw working. "Fine. Outside." He nods towards the door. He steps back, allowing Ryan to gather his things and stand. He nods at us, his eyes sliding over me. Then he freezes.

Shit.

"Ms. Carmichael," the deputy says, pointing at me, then at Ryan with the end of his pen, his gaze moving back and forth between us.

Ryan has stopped dead in his tracks.

"You two know each other?" he asks.

Zoe's fingers are now cutting off my circulation, but I welcome it. The pain anchors me to the present. Otherwise, I think I might faint.

"Yes," I manage. The word is strangled. I'm not even lying and yet I sound guilty as hell.

"Hmm," he says, his brown eyes flicking to Brandon, then Zoe, then back to me. He nods, and I can tell I haven't heard the end of this.

Ryan and Deputy Romano stand outside in the parking lot alongside his sheriff's vehicle, talking. Ryan has his arms crossed before him, Deputy Romano's hand is hooked on his belt. Right above his gun.

"Anyone read lips?" Zoe asks weakly.

I shake my head. "I'd give my left kidney to be able to."

"It'll be fine," Brandon says. I'm beginning to take his measure. Sunny optimism is his jam. He lowers his voice. "We fixed up the truck."

"Did anyone else see you do it?" I ask.

Brandon shakes his head. "We did it in my dad's shop. No one's the wiser."

"What do you think he'll say?" I chew on my lip. Deputy Romano's investigation has thrown a wrench in the whole business. I feel bad for my sister's family, I do. They do deserve to know what happened to their daughter. But I also deserve a curse-free existence. As do the rest of my sisters. Breaking the curse has to be the priority here.

"He's good under pressure," Brandon says. "He'll think of something."

My phone buzzes and I jump. It's a text from my mom. A GIF of a clock. I knew I shouldn't have shown her how to use that feature.

"I need to get home." I close my laptop, throwing it in my bag.

"Let's wait," Zoe says. "What if Deputy Romano stops you on your way out? We need to get our stories straight with Ryan."

I nod.

Headlights flood the coffee shop, and I blink, squinting into the bright. It's Ryan's truck. The deputy must be done talking to him.

"Mer, he's coming back in," Zoe says. I can see she's paralyzed with fear. But by some miracle, I spring into action. I grab my phone and haul ass for the bathroom, locking the door as the bell chimes again.

"What did you tell him?" I text Ryan furiously. I'm sure the police can search our phones if they really want, but right now all I care about is knowing what the hell to tell Deputy Romano.

Three little dots undulate as I pace the confines of the bathroom.

"Truth," Ryan's text pops up.

I goggle at the phone, collapsing against the tiled wall. "?!?" I text back.

Those infernal dots blink again…

"Today 1st day we met—B+Z set up. Camping B4, no reception."

That fast-thinking mofo. I blow out a breath, shoving my phone in my pocket. I flush the toilet and run my hands under the water. I can do this.

Deputy Romano is sitting next to Zoe, chatting with Brandon. Brandon laughs at something he's just said, as if they're long-lost besties. Zoe's quieter, her smile weak. I slide into the seat next to Brandon.

"I was just telling Brandon I played baseball for Summit back in the day." Deputy Romano smiles. "Pitcher."

"Cool," I manage.

"Ryan was a pitcher until last year," Brandon offers. I know he's trying to endear Ryan to the deputy, but I wish he hadn't brought him up. I don't want Ryan under Deputy Romano's scrutiny any more than necessary. "Kid has a cannon. I swore he was going to play college ball, maybe go all the way."

"He doesn't play anymore?" Deputy Romano asks.

Brandon shakes his head. "His grandpa passed away, and he quit to help out his gran. She needs some help, and he didn't want to be traveling for games so much. And he got a job to help pay the bills."

"Tough break," Deputy Romano says. I agree. I feel doubly bad that my misdirected kidnapping efforts kept him from his grandma. Deputy Romano turns his attention on me. "How are you holding up, Meriah?"

I bob my head. "Okay, I guess."

"I wasn't aware you and Mr. Kearney knew each other."

I shrug. "We don't, really. Brandon and Zoe got the wild idea to, like, set us up. It was just coffee."

"A double date?" the deputy asks.

"It's not exactly like that—"

"We're just friends—"

Brandon and Zoe talk over each other, competing for the role of reddest junior at the table. You could cut the awkwardness with a knife.

Deputy Romano holds up his hands. "I'm sorry I asked." He looks back at me. "You remember anything else you'd like to share?"

I shake my head, swallowing. "I'd tell you if I did."

He nods, standing. "Good. You kids have a good night."

And then he leaves, taking what's left of my frayed nerves with him.

The coiled tension in my body doesn't unwind until we're safely in Zoe's car and halfway home. I feel as brittle as a dry leaf. Deputy Romano is yet another complication to add to our already Herculean quest. It's moments like this that I really wish I were old enough to drink.

Mom and Dad are waiting, lecture in hand, when I walk through the front door. But when I tell them that it was Deputy Romano who waylaid me and made me late, their anger fizzles like an old balloon.

I finally collapse on my bed, kicking off my shoes, when my phone buzzes.

I whip it out. It's Ryan. "U ok?" he asks.

"Yup. Told DR the truth," I text back, resisting putting *truth* in quotes.

"Good."

I wait. Good? That's it?

He texts again. "Any ideas for how to find Z?" I know by Z he means Zeus, not Zoe.

I smack my forehead, a smile growing on my face. In my terror over Deputy Romano's reappearance, I'd totally forgotten my earlier epiphany.

"Yup," I say, adding a smiley. "Free tomorrow?"

CHAPTER 20

Her name is Sibyll Ambrosia. She's a history professor with a focus on Greek mythology and the author of the textbook Ryan pilfered from his school library. As soon as I saw her name, I knew that she's more than a mere teacher. Sibyls are prophets and oracles, keepers of knowledge and wisdom. While there was originally one sibyl, back in the era of gods and Titans, the word transformed into a title as the years passed. The Order of the Sibyls has continued, though their numbers have dwindled. I can't believe I didn't think of it before. If there's anyone who can tell us where Zeus is, it'd be a sibyl.

And even better, she works at Oregon State University, a blessed two-hours' drive from us. I can hardly believe our good fortune.

"How do you know she's really a sibyl and not just named that?" Ryan asks. We're sitting in his truck, chugging down Highway 20. After I explained my theory, Ryan and I decided to make a trip to see her. Some questions just don't translate into an email. Brandon had a game today, and Zoe has her SAT prep class, so it's just Ryan and me. I try not to think about how nervous that makes me feel. Nervous and excited.

"I just feel it," I say. "She's a Greek Studies professor, for god's sake. It's our best theory."

"It's our only theory…" he jokes.

"Hey, I don't see you coming up with any bright ideas."

He chuckles. "One point to the lady."

We haven't talked about Deputy Romano or his investigation, and I'm too chicken-shit to raise the topic with Ryan. I don't want to spook him, to make him think I'm worried he'll turn us in. I'm not exactly worried about that, not anymore. I'm worried the police will link him to the accident. That he'll be arrested. Not worried. Terrified.

The radio crackles angrily and Ryan reaches to change it, spinning the dial. It's one of those old-timey ones you'd see in a period movie from the fifties.

"You really need to get an MP3 player in here."

"It'd ruin the effect."

"I forgot how crackly static is a favorite feature in classic cars."

"You have to pay extra for it in some states." He nods sagely.

"How'd you end up with this truck?" I ask.

"It was my grandpa's. Gran said I could have it if I fixed it up and got it running again."

"How long'd it take you?" I want to ask him what happened to his grandfather, but I think it might be too personal.

"About two years," he admits. "Brandon's older brother Adam is good with cars; he helped me out a bunch."

"It's a real sonuvabitch to drive," I admit.

He glances over, amused. "I'm sorry to not provide a more convenient vehicle for my kidnapping." His look warms me, making me want to roll down the window and hang my head out the side. I ignore how his hand is resting on the seat between us. How I could put mine down right next to it, how our pinkies would touch, sending that electric spark through me again—

"I'm actually impressed that you could drive it," Ryan admits, cutting off my spiraling thoughts. "The clutch is really temperamental. Not many kids our age can drive stick."

"My dad taught me to. He thought it was an important life skill to have. Like changing a tire—"

"Or rewinding a VHS tape?"

I laugh. "Well, he was right, wasn't he? It turned out to be extremely useful. I picked it up quickly anyway. I remember from past lives."

"Really?" he asks. "You remember that much detail?"

"The newer lives are fresher," I admit. "The old ones are foggier, like looking through a dirty window. But yeah, over a few years, they all came back to me for the most part. Though the parts about my sisters are stronger." I leave out that the parts about him are stronger, too.

"That must have been hard."

I let out a little laugh. "It was not awesome. I think my parents were about a day away from committing me." My tone is light, but I swallow at the memory. Even now, the memory of my fear that they would send me away squeezes my lungs in its vise grip. I'm not sure I would have been able to forgive them for that.

"How did you get a handle on it?" Ryan asks.

"It wasn't until I went back to the beginning. I kind of cycled through my lifetimes backwards from modern times. It wasn't until the end when I finally realized who I was. Merope. When I understood what had happened. It was like…" I try to explain. "Anchoring into myself. Suddenly, I had context. I got it. It was a lot easier from then on."

"Do you still have the visions of old times?"

"Not much. Occasionally. Now my visions are mostly of the future."

"Just about your sisters or other stuff?"

"Other stuff sometimes. I get a lot of déjà vu. I was able to save my cousin from choking once. And find Zoe's dog when it was lost. If not for all the killing stuff, it'd be a pretty cool gift."

"If not for all the killing stuff," he echoes.

"How about you?" I ask. "You only remember during your seizures?"

He glances at me sharply. "First, no one knows about those seizures. No one except Gran and Brandon. You cannot tell anyone else."

I nod. "I won't."

He takes a deep breath. "I only see things during the seizures. And I think I started the other way from you. I saw Orion first—that lifetime. And Zeus and the Pleiades. Your sisters. I remember you. I had a bit of a thing for you." He glances over at me quickly.

My breath hitches as I paw through those memories, trying to find any indication that what he said is true. There's not much. We barely interacted with Orion. Maybe I spoke with him once, at a banquet before it all went wrong... "What?" I stumble over my thoughts. "I was like...seventeen."

"I was only in my early twenties! Times were different back then. All your sisters were beautiful, but there was something about you. Something...alive. Do you remember dancing with me at Artemis's harvest festival?"

I pause, scanning again. "I don't think so..." I trail off, kicking myself for not noticing. For not remembering. How could his soul have passed beneath my notice?

"It's okay," he says. "You had tons of admirers. And there

was a lot of wine flowing, if I remember. Dionysus was in full force."

That brings it back. "*Oh…I* don't think I remembered much from that night. Not just you."

"I'm slightly less offended."

I scoff, desperate to change the mood between us. It feels too real, and I'm not sure I can continue without saying or doing something stupid. Like threading my fingers through his. "If you were so taken with me, why'd you shoot me with an arrow? Is that, like, the Greek equivalent of pulling a girl's pigtail on the playground?"

"I could shoot a soaring hawk out of the sky. I was the greatest archer the world has ever seen. You never wondered why when I shot at you from ten feet away, I missed?"

I think on that. "But you didn't miss. You hit me."

"I thought Zeus was going to order me to kill all of you. So I shot you in the most non-lethal spot I could manage to incapacitate you. I was hoping he would forget about you."

My eyes widen slightly. I can't be around Ryan without more pieces falling into place. I can't help feeling like everything I was so sure of was completely and totally wrong.

"Oh, this exit." I point, and Ryan veers the truck, prompting an angry honk from the Subaru in the next lane. The drive has passed so quickly, I can hardly believe it.

"Sorry," Ryan mutters, but we make the exit to Corvallis.

We're going to the sibyl's house, as it's Saturday. It'd be better to find her at her office, but we don't exactly have five free hours to make the drive here and back on a school day. So Zoe had one of her tech-savvy student body friends do a little sleuthing, and we came up with her home address. I shove down my worry over what happens if she won't see us. Or if she doesn't know what we're talking about.

I use my phone to navigate Ryan through the winding streets and towards the sibyl's house. She lives in the outskirts of Corvallis. As we get closer, I see that it's a nice neighborhood of big houses with broad, sloping lawns leading down to the Willamette River.

"It's nice here," Ryan says.

"Yeah, my dad's a Beaver," I say. "He wants me to go to OSU."

"What do *you* want?" Ryan asks.

I shrug. "Not sure yet. Part of me would love to get out of Oregon, but I'll apply here and U of O. Hard to beat in-state tuition. What about you?"

"Perfect world, I would have gotten a baseball scholarship and gone somewhere warm and exotic. That's not an option anymore, and there aren't a ton of archery scholarships to be had. Reality, I'll probably go to Central."

"The community college?" I ask.

He nods. "I'm gonna learn to code."

"Really? I wouldn't peg you for a computer geek."

"You think I should be a construction worker or something?" His tone is light, but I can tell he's offended.

"That's not what I meant—"

"It's okay. It'd be a logical path for me. I don't love the idea of sitting at a desk all day, but I don't want to work in the cold until my body breaks down. I want to find something where I can have security. Take care of Gran. She won't be able to live on her own forever. And in Seattle and Portland they give out programming jobs like candy."

"Smart," I say, impressed by his maturity. His willingness to sacrifice. Most kids I know, myself included, are still dicking around, worrying about who to take to junior prom or whether they'll make state this year. Ryan's planning for his future.

"The turn is up here on the left," I say, pointing at the driveway. It's long and winding, shadowed by tall evergreen trees.

The house comes into view. It's a gorgeous craftsman with red trim and a red door, with a big back porch paralleling the cut of the river. Down past the sloping green lawn, a dock juts out into the river. A jolt of recognition hits me. I've seen this dock before. It's where my sister dies.

"We need to leave," I breathe.

Ryan puts the truck in park and turns to face me. "What the hell are you talking about?"

"I've seen this place before in one of my visions. Alcyone drowns here."

"You had another vision?" Ryan narrows his eyes. "Why didn't you tell me?"

"I don't know." I flail my hands. "It's not like I'm used to having an ally."

"From now on, Mer, no secrets, okay? If we're going to do this together, we need to trust each other."

I nod, wondering if the fact that I think his eyes are the crystal blue of Lake Tahoe counts as a secret I must disclose. I decide not.

"Tell me the vision—exactly."

I do, relating to him what I remember. Alcyone floating off the dock.

"It happens near the water," he finally says. "As long as I don't go anywhere near the river, it'll be fine, right?"

I give a half-hearted murmur of agreement. The Fates

pull at Ryan like the most powerful magnet. Even if we turned and drove away right now, I'm not sure it would be enough to stop what has been destined.

"Come on, Mer. This is our only lead. We've come all this way. We can't turn around without at least talking to the sibyl."

I chew on my lip, my thoughts racing.

Knuckles rap on my window and I screech, jerking against my seatbelt. My hand flies to my chest as I look and see that it's her. Sibyll Ambrosia. I grab the crank and roll down the window slowly.

"Can I help you?" she asks. She looks like her picture, with the large glasses and dark curls pulled back into a loose ponytail. But today she wears black leggings and a loose denim shirt and has gardening gloves on. Her face is pretty, her skin olive-toned, her nose severe in a way that suits her. She's younger than I expected. Perhaps in her late thirties or early forties.

"We're high school students," I manage. "We have a... Greek history project we're working on. I know it's the weekend, but we were hoping to ask you a few questions."

She purses her lips. "There's little I can tell you that you can't find on Wikipedia. I don't mean to be rude, but it wouldn't be very scholarly of me to do your project for you. Much of the learning comes from the experience of doing the research yourself. I'm afraid I can't help you."

She turns to leave and Ryan leans over me. "It's not a project. It's personal. Are you a sibyl?"

Her head curves back around, her features schooled to neutrality. She lets out a little laugh. "My name is Sibyll, so I guess I am one."

I shake my head, looking her dead in the eyes. "No. Are you a sibyl?"

She cocks her head, putting her gloved hands on her hips.

"Who are you?" Behind her glasses, I think I see something. A flash of something old. A recognition. But then it's gone so fast that I'm not sure it wasn't my imagination.

I suck in a breath. "I'm Merope. This is Orion."

Her mouth opens slightly as she looks between us. Ryan is still leaning over me, his scent of hay and starlight tickling my nose. Finally, she shuts it. "Why don't you both come in?"

The inside of the sibyl's house is clean and bright, with large windows oriented to let in the view of the river. Plush rugs grace the polished hardwood floor, and we settle on a thick leather couch at Sibyll's request. Bookshelves line the wall filled with ancient-looking tomes. Over the fireplace is a black and orange vase decorated with Greek warriors in battle. It looks real. Old.

"You guys want anything to drink? LaCroix?" she asks. "I have pretty much every flavor."

"Pamplemousse for me," I say.

She looks at Ryan expectantly.

"Lime," he finally says, as if he's embarrassed to admit he even knows what the flavor options are.

I snort, looking sideways at him. "Your secret is safe with me."

He nudges me with his elbow. "Oh, whatever, Ms. Pamplemousse." He says the word with a phony French accent that makes me giggle.

"What? That's the name of the flavor."

"Can't just say grapefruit like a normal human being. You have to be all fancy."

"What's the point of drinking fancy water if you can't be fancy?" I point out.

He rolls his eyes, which I take as a victory. Point, Mer.

Sibyll hands us our drinks and settles into the leather armchair across from us. She has a coconut LaCroix in her hand. Didn't know anyone chose that one on purpose.

"So. Orion and Merope. Not exactly the most modern of names," she says. "Your parents Greek history buffs?"

I swallow. Might as well wade right into it. "Those aren't our names—in this lifetime."

She raises an eyebrow.

"You in the mood for a story?" I chuckle nervously.

"Why not?"

I briefly sketch out the history of our many lifetimes, Ryan filling in a few details.

When I finally fall silent, Sibyll examines us both with sharp eyes. "That's quite a tale."

"We thought that the sibyls might be able to help us locate Zeus. So we can beseech him to lift the curse. Will you help us?" I ask.

She taps her chin with a finger. "If what you say is true, you'd have knowledge what most other high schoolers wouldn't. How many columns did Artemis's temple in Athens have?"

Ryan and I exchange a glance. Artemis didn't have a temple in Athens. It was a trick question.

Ryan gives me a small nod. He's reached the same conclusion.

"None. There was no temple in Athens. It was located in Ephesus."

Sibyll inclines her head. "Which was the most important Ancient Greek festival?"

"Depends on which god you ask," Ryan says. "But in my opinion, it was the Panathenaia."

The Panathenaia were week-long festivals that celebrated the birth of the goddess Athena, goddess of wisdom and craft.

"A fair answer," Sibyll says, tucking her legs up underneath her in her chair. "All right. Let's say I believe you. What do you want me to do about it?"

"The sibyls are keepers of knowledge and wisdom. We need to find Zeus and convince him to help us. If you could tell us where he is, how to find him, that would be huge."

"And make an introduction," Ryan adds. "If you know anyone in his court."

Sibyll's face softens. "I'm sorry to be the one to tell you this. You guys seem like nice kids. But there's nothing I can do to help you. Zeus is dead."

CHAPTER 22

It's like she's punched me in the gut. All the wind has gone out of me. The words ring in my ears. In my soul. *Zeus is dead.* Now we'll never be free.

"How?" Ryan asks. His voice is faint.

"*When* is the better question," Sibyll says. "And the answer is a thousand years ago. When people stopped believing, they began to fade away."

I shake my head, trying to clear the ringing. "I don't understand."

"Gods exist to be worshipped. Their life force is derived from the energy of humanity's prayers and petitions, their adoration. When people began to turn away to other religions, like Christianity, the Olympian dynasty began to wither."

"That doesn't make sense." Ryan frowns. "The gods existed before humanity, together with the Titans. The gods created humans."

She shakes her head. "That's the myth, created by humanity to justify their belief in a higher power with control over them."

"But…the gods were complete dicks to the early humans," I say. "Prometheus was punished for eternity just for giving them fire so they wouldn't freeze to death. Why would humans make up the idea of cosmic overlords?"

"The world is a scary, dangerous place, full of unknowns. It was a comfort to humanity to believe that there was something bigger than themselves in control. It's easier to deceive yourself into beseeching a higher power than to step into your own."

That makes a sort of twisted sense.

"Why didn't we disappear then?" Ryan asks. "When the gods faded away. We're still here."

"Well, Orion was human," Sibyll says. "I'm not sure about Merope. Perhaps the curse bound you to the world, so you endured."

"It doesn't make sense that the curse could endure when the power behind it vanished."

Sibyll shrugs. "I don't have all the answers, guys. I've never heard of a situation like yours. But if I were speculating, I would say that the curse didn't emanate from Zeus. It came from the scythe. And it's possible that an object of power like the scythe still endures. It was created by the gods —imbued with their magic—but it was a physical object. Many of those still exist even today. That's part of why the order of the sibyls continues on. To locate and manage such items."

I seize upon her comment, a spark of hope kindling in the fog of my despair. "So the scythe might still exist."

She nods. "It probably does."

I look at Ryan excitedly. "Maybe that's all we need to break the curse. Maybe we don't need Zeus at all."

"Okay. Do you know where it is?" he asks Sibyll.

"I would suspect it's still on Mount Olympus, though I can't know for sure."

"Mount Olympus still exists?" I ask.

"Like I said, much of the physical infrastructure built by the gods still remains. That includes buildings. Though Olympus is hidden well."

I lean forwards eagerly. "How do we get to Olympus?"

Sibyll looks between us. "No mortal has gone there for a very long time. It's a dangerous place."

"No more dangerous than this stupid curse," Ryan mutters.

"What type of danger?" I ask, more cautious. I'm eager to break the curse, but it won't do us any good if we get killed. Who knows what Ryan and I will remember in our next lives? It might take us years to remember that we're not enemies. Not to mention, I'm rather fond of this life and am growing fonder by the day.

"Boobytraps, I'm sure," Sibyll explains. "When the gods were fading from this world, they gathered their treasures to them and locked themselves inside their fortress at Olympus. They feared that their enemies would want to take advantage of their weakness and attack. So they sealed it off, and then partially phased it out of this reality so no one would stumble upon it.

"This is sounding better and better," Ryan says wryly.

I study her, cocking my head. "The sibyls were part of it, weren't they?"

She nods. "We were tasked as the final keepers of the resting place of the gods and their lore. It's only our order who knows the location of Olympus and how to access it."

"So I guess we're pretty lucky we came here to talk to you," I say.

"Will you help us get into Olympus?" Ryan asks.

She shakes her head. "It'd be irresponsible of me to let you go. You're just kids. I don't know what you'd face in there."

"If we don't go, more girls will die young," I say. "In this lifetime and the next. Please."

Ryan chimes in. "We're willing to risk our lives if it means ending this. And we're not helpless. I'm as good an archer in this life as I was as Orion."

I raise an eyebrow at the boast, but I've seen the trophies on his shelf. Besides, Ryan doesn't really seem like the bragging type.

Sibyll pushes to her feet, walking to her bookshelf. She stands before it, seeming to be thinking. Finally, she retrieves a book, returning to her chair. She sits for a moment, stroking the cover. Finally, she nods to herself and looks up at us. "I believe what you're saying. I can sense your ancient selves in both of you. The Fates clearly brought you to me. I'm not sure I should stand in your way."

She offers the book, and Ryan takes it. We both look at the title, our shoulders brushing together. *Greek Tragedies.* Ryan opens the cover, and my eyes widen. A portion of the interior pages have been cut out to leave a hiding place. An ancient key is nestled inside.

"This key unlocks the gate to Mount Olympus. I'm granting you permission to use it *only* for the purpose of locating the scythe and breaking the curse. When you complete your task, you must return it to me." Her words are forceful, and goosebumps rise on my arms. She's speaking some sort of spell over us. I feel like Aladdin getting instructions before he heads into the tiger's mouth to retrieve the lamp.

"Your terms are acceptable," Ryan says, and the authority in his voice startles me. I hear Orion in those words.

"So, where exactly is the door?" I ask. *Please don't be in Athens, please don't be in Athens*, I think.

"In Athens," Sibyll replies.

Damn.

"But there's another way to get there. A…place of transit, if you will. We call it the Byway."

Oh, thank god. I'm pretty good at wrapping Dad around my little finger, but a spontaneous family trip to Greece would be a stretch, even for me. Creepy sounding Byway for the win!

"Olympus sits atop the Mytikas peak in central Greece. But all mountaintops are mythical places, charged with the same energy. You can reach Olympus from any dominant peak. I believe the closest to here would be Mount Shasta."

Shasta was in Northern California. That could work. "What do we look for? Shasta is a big mountain."

"The key will show you the way," Sibyll says. "But once you're in Olympus, it'll be up to you to find the scythe and break the curse. I have no wisdom to offer you regarding either of those subjects."

"It's okay," I say. "You've been so helpful. I can't believe how much closer we are. I can't thank you enough."

Ryan is silent beside me, and I nudge him to get him to chime in with his thanks as well. I look over and I see that he's no longer listening. He's staring out the window, riveted by something outside.

"Ryan?" I put my hand on his knee and give it a little shake. "You okay?"

He surges to his feet. "There's someone in the river," he says. "I think she's drowning."

CHAPTER 23

Ryan is out through the glass patio doors and on the deck before my brain catches up.

"Don't!" I call after him, cursing under my breath.

"What?" Sibyll asks, alarmed.

"We can't let him near the water," I say, following him outside. But it's likely too late. Things are already in motion.

"You had a vision?" Sibyll asks, jogging next to me.

"Yes." I'm breathless with fear. "Of Alcyone dead, floating in water."

Sibyll blanches beside me.

Ryan is out on the dock now, and we meet him at the end.

"Hey!" He's calling at the girl, waving his hands, peering into the sunshine flickering off the river to try to determine if she's flailing or drowning.

"That's my neighbor's daughter," Sibyll says. "She swims in the river all the time. She's a strong swimmer."

The swimmer has caught sight of us and has turned our direction, headed towards us with sure strokes.

I grab Ryan's elbow and pull him back from the edge as she approaches, clinging to him with fingers as cold as ice, despite the warm day. I don't want him anywhere near that girl. We shouldn't even be on this dock.

She reaches the ladder at the end of Sibyll's dock and pulls herself up. She's a pretty blonde about our age in a sleek speedo and swim cap. She lifts her goggles, which have left rings around her green eyes. I recognize that face. My stomach heaves and I think I might throw up.

"Hey, Ms. A," she says brightly.

"Hello, Melanie," Sibyll replies.

"I saw you waving. Everything okay?" Melanie asks. She's scrutinizing Ryan with an appreciative eye, and I suddenly understand why she was so eager to come over here and "investigate." A thread of jealousy snakes through me, low and hot. I adjust my grip on Ryan's arm so it looks like we're just out for a stroll, rather than me holding him back from a terrible but certain fate.

Ryan clears his throat. "Sorry. Didn't mean to interrupt your workout. I saw someone in the river and thought something was wrong."

"Nope, everything's just fine. I was finishing up."

"Great," he replies. "Well, we don't want to keep you."

With what I think I recognize as a flash of disappointment, Melanie smiles. "All right then. Have a good one." She heads back towards the ladder and I turn to Ryan, reluctantly releasing his arm. "Ohmygod," I whisper to him. "I think we just avoided fate."

Ryan grins at me, and my heart pools like melted butter in my chest. "See, nothing to worry about." He threads his arm around me and pulls me to the warm expanse of his body in a side hug. "Maybe we just needed to be a team all along."

I'm still smiling when I feel him stiffen against me. A croaking sound escapes him, and I don't understand what's happening. Until he starts to shake.

His arm slides from me as he falls towards the weathered boards of the dock. I try to catch him, but my body is sluggish to respond, not willing to recognize what's happening. He's having a seizure.

I drop to my knees just as one of his feet thrashes out, catching me in the stomach. The air whooshes out of me and I fall back on my ass, temporarily stunned. It's too late when I realize how close to the edge of the dock he is. How he's going to tumble over the edge.

"Ryan!" I hear myself scream his name as he goes over the side, my own voice a foreign sound in my ears. I feel like my senses are closing around me, my body a prison of bright sunlight and shaky breath and the sharp taste of my fear. My body is a sluggish foe rebelling against my direction.

Sibyll is faster and is already at the edge of the dock where Ryan fell when I finally find my way to hands and knees and scramble to meet her. A sliver pierces my palm, but I'm barely aware. Ryan is seizing. In the river. There's no way he won't take water into his lungs. He could die.

"He's having a seizure!" Sibyll yells to Melanie, who's turned around at the commotion. She hasn't made it far from our dock and is now swimming back towards him as fast as she can.

Thank the gods he's faceup in the water, but his body keeps dipping down below the lapping waves, his eyes back in his head, his face as pale as a corpse's. This doesn't make sense. My vision was of her, not him.

Melanie has reached him now and is making to swim around behind him. But one of his arms flings out like a tree trunk and catches her straight in the face, stunning her. She falls back in the water, and I see the red of blood coming from her nose.

"Oh my god," I say, pulling off my shoes. Sibyll is doing the same.

"I'll get him, you get her," is all she says before she leaps off the dock into the river.

I follow suit, feeling that peculiar lightness of falling before I plunge into the water, the cold of the river like a slap to my face. I kick my feet and surface, seeing my target.

Sibyll has almost reached Ryan already; it looks like his seizure is slowing.

I reach Melanie and see her eyes are closed. I can't tell if she's breathing or if she's inhaled water. I swim around the back of her, threading my arms through her armpits and kicking towards shore. I'm only an average swimmer, but adrenaline surges through me, and my toes touch the pebbles of the river's bottom in just a few seconds.

Melanie's weight settles upon me as we emerge from the river, and I overbalance, falling onto my ass with her in my lap. I scramble up and pull her another few feet, the rocks of the shore gouging into the soles of my feet.

I collapse to the ground with her. Sibyll has done the same with Ryan, making it slightly farther up the bank to shore. I can't concern myself with him right now—I focus on Melanie. Alcyone. Blood trickles from her nose where Ryan hit her, and it doesn't look like she's breathing.

Grateful for that PE class where Coach Donaldson brought in a CPR instructor, I position my hands below her diaphragm and begin pumping. *Come on, come on.*

I pinch her nose and blow air into her mouth, the copper tang of her blood filling my nostrils.

I start pumping again and her eyes flutter open as she coughs, water bubbling out of her mouth. I roll her gently onto her side, letting her cough out the rest of the water from her lungs.

Ryan groans and my eyes snap up, taking in the sight of him pushing gingerly to a seated position, his head cradled in his hands.

Sibyll slumps back onto her hip, brushing her wet hair out of her eyes.

"You're okay," I say to Melanie. Relief hits me like a freight train. Everyone is okay. We bested the Fates today. Even as the thought flares in my mind, I try to douse it, to hide it so it will never reach those immortal puppetmasters, so they're not angered by my defiance. I wouldn't put it above the petty bitches to strike Melanie with a bolt of lightning from a clear blue sky.

Without a word, Sibyll and I exchange places, she helping Melanie up the bank onto the softer grass, me settling at Ryan's side.

He's lying back in the grass, gazing at the sky.

"I almost killed her," he finally says hoarsely.

"Key word *almost*," I reply with mock levity. Somehow I recognize that if he's going to be the fatalistic one, it's up to me to be optimistic. He grabs my hand and pulls it against his chest, letting it rest against his wet shirt. I ignore the roaring of my heart.

"She'll be okay. Don't feel bad. It was an accident."

"It always is," he says, still not meeting my eye.

Isn't that the truth.

The drive home is subdued.

After helping Melanie back to her parents' house, where the girl promises she'll go straight to urgent care to get checked out, Sibyll feeds us sandwiches and gives us something to wear while our clothes tumble in the dryer.

I give her a hug when we leave, the book with its key tucked safely under Ryan's arm. She's given us so much. Hospitality, hope. And she helped me save Alcyone. I didn't know it was possible to owe someone so much after just one day.

I stare out the window on the drive home, thinking about the feel of Ryan's hand fixed in mine. The terror I felt as I saw him go into the water. It's not just that I can't do this without him. It's that I don't want to. Something has been growing in me that's undeniable, and I don't know what to do. I've never had a boyfriend, so there's the normal teenage paralysis when it comes to the prospect of dating. Sure, I've got fuzzy experience from past lives, but those memories are like watching something on TV. Plus, everything is different in this lifetime of social media and texting. My mind drifts, imagining life after all this is over. If we really manage to break the curse. Would I never see Ryan again? Would we go through all this together and then simply part ways? Is that what he would want? I want to ask him, but I'm a coward.

So I simply wave goodbye when he drops me off, promising to text him to plan our trip to Shasta.

I feign perkiness to Mom and Dad, who've ordered Thai food. I mow down some chicken pad thai and give them a seriously abridged version of my trip to Corvallis. I told them we were going to do research for a project at the OSU library. I mean, there was a grain of truth in there, right?

They settle in to watch Netflix, and I head to bed. My body is sluggish with shock, and I want nothing more than to take a scalding shower and wash the scent of the river and Melanie's blood from me.

Sleep seizes me in a powerful grip, dragging me down into blackness.

But my night is not restful.

It's full of dreams—being swept out into the ocean by a powerful current, battling Zeus and his lackeys. Reaching Olympus to open the book, only to find that the key is gone. My subconscious is a master at inventing fears I haven't even thought of yet.

I tumble through them all until I find myself standing in a throne room. The room orients around me, coming into focus. Tall marble pillars march in parallel lines, the floor inset with delicate mosaic scenes of the gods. The ceiling soars above us, painted with colorful frescoes of the bright Grecian sky. This isn't a dream. It's a vision. Then I realize the nature of my thoughts. Us? Who's us? I'm alone in this room, yet I know I'm not. Ryan's here too. Somewhere. Or he's supposed to be.

"Ryan?" I call out. My voice echoes, swallowed by the cavernous space.

As I scan the room for any sign of him, my eyes catch on something out of place. A boot—sticking out from behind a pillar. No, not a boot. A booted foot.

"Ryan!" I scream as I run for it, desperate to see, yet terrified at what's waiting for me. The dichotomy steals my breath.

I skid to a halt on the polished tile floor, and a moan escapes me. "No, no, no!" I fall to my knees beside Ryan, my hands fluttering about his face.

He lies in a pool of burgundy blood. A jagged wound on his forearm gapes at me, and something about it looks animal—savage. Like he's been mauled. More blood blooms on his shoulder and thigh. His blue eyes stare vacantly skyward, his mouth slightly agape.

The heat of a tear streaks down my face, dripping off my chin. "What happened?" I whisper, taking one of his hands in mine.

He's cold—stiff—but I ignore the unpleasant sensation. His forearm is slashed with wounds, too, and I examine them. They look like puncture marks.

"What did this to you?" I ask, but he doesn't answer. My heart keens within me at the prospect of him being gone—leaving me alone in this place. I see this future and I don't even know if we broke the curse. What if by going into Olympus, the only thing we accomplish is getting Ryan killed?

I reach up gently and close his eyes, my fingertips lingering on his cheek. Feeling against the feathers of his long lashes, the prickly stubble on his cheek. Things I found myself wanting to do in life, but I would only get to do in death. I lean forwards slowly and press a soft kiss to his lips. A tear drips off my nose, shimmering like a diamond on his pale skin. "Goodbye."

I move to stand and jerk awake, the sensation of being

ripped out of my vision throwing off my equilibrium. The room spins around me, and I find my sheet is drenched. I pull my other pillow towards me and curl around it, releasing a muffled sob. Ryan is going to die. We need to abort this whole sordid business. I can't ask him to sacrifice himself to break the curse. The irony is not lost on me. Two days ago, a vision of Ryan's death would have filled me with powerful relief. Now, my mind races for a way to stop it.

I curse the Fates. God, they're such bitches! Then a thought strikes me. If the Olympians have faded away, are the Fates gone too? Have I been pissed at a trio of old ladies who don't even exist anymore? When it's all just random chance? No. I reject the idea. The Fates aren't gods, after all, not like Zeus and Chronos. Besides, the orchestration of my misery is too perfect. There's got to be some power up there pulling the strings.

My stomach rumbles. Guess that pad thai didn't stay with me too long. I wipe my eyes and sit up. It's only 10:30. I've hardly been in bed for an hour.

I pad downstairs, hoping to prowl the kitchen for a snack. There's no way I'm going to be able to sleep with my mind racing like it is. Mom and Dad are curled up on the couch, her head on his chest, his arm around her shoulder. The news is on in the background, the volume low. I can't decide if it's cute or sickening how they seem gravitate towards each other when I'm not looking. Like they don't want me to know they still love each other.

"Can't sleep, sweetie?" Mom looks over her shoulder as I open the refrigerator, grabbing some Greek yogurt.

"Bad dream," I offer.

That alarms both my parents, and my dad puts the TV on mute. "Need to talk about it?" he asks. Back when I was first getting my visions, I would be pretty distraught after them. I don't blame my parents for having a bit of PTSD on the subject of my dream life.

"It's okay." I shake my head as I retrieve the box of granola and pour it into a bowl.

They look skeptical.

"Really, I'm fine," I insist. For a moment, I let myself daydream about what they'd say if I told them the truth. About everything. My seer abilities, past lives. Ryan, the curse. The scythe. But I worry they'd put me away. When you grow up, you seem to lose your ability to believe in anything at all out of the ordinary. This would be no exception. I can't risk it, not when I'm so close. Maybe on their deathbeds or something.

I sink onto the other end of the couch, stirring my granola and yogurt. I'd grabbed what was left of the blueberries, too.

Mom smiles at me. "Maybe we should go away for a weekend, just the three of us," she says. "Out to the coast maybe?"

"Sounds great." I manage a smile. A face on the TV catches my eye, and I freeze, spoon halfway to my mouth. "Hey, turn that up."

My dad unmutes the TV and the news anchor's serious voice fills the living room. "...passed away today after nearly drowning in Willamette River, near her family home. Medical examiners have indicated that the cause of Melanie's death is currently unknown..." The rest of the words are lost to me. A roaring sound fills my ears, a numbness overtaking me.

"Sweetie?"

A hand touches my shoulder and I jerk, my eyes focusing on my mom.

"You okay?" she asks.

"I know her," I manage.

"Really?" Dad asks. "Didn't she live in Corvallis?"

"Track," I manage. My god. Melanie—Alcyone is dead. Even though we did everything right—we *saved* her. Somehow, she died anyway. My despair is heavy within me, pulling me down like a weight. The curse is ironclad. They *always* die. I knew that. That was why I'd set out to kill Ryan in the first place. Idiot. Why had I let myself hope?

A calm certainty settles over me.

"Poor Mer," my mom says. "You've had a hard week." She doesn't say it, but I know she's thinking of Electra, who died in the car accident.

I shake my head, summoning my composure. "I didn't know her well. It's just sad," I say. "Would it be okay if Zoe and I go camping next weekend? Somewhere close. I think it would help me clear my head to get away. Have some fun."

"Nature is the best cure," Dad says. "I think it's a great idea."

Mom looks at him and I can tell she's less thrilled with the idea of me going off unsupervised. But Dad's already spoken, and one thing they don't do is contradict each other in front of me.

"Sure, sweetie." Mom reaches out and strokes my curls. "Camping's a great idea. Somewhere close."

"Thanks." I settle into Mom's side, and we're all three nestled into each other. I'm struck, not for the first time, by how glad I am that people can't read each other's thoughts. Because Zoe and I won't be camping nearby, and we won't be alone. We'll be headed to Mount Shasta. And then, Olympus.

CHAPTER 25

The trip comes together fairly effortlessly, actually.

I spent much of the ride home from Sibyll's house planning how the hell I was going to get to Mount Shasta without my parents knowing. The only thing I came up with was the camping trip with Zoe. Plus, the thought of being alone with Ryan overnight again makes my stomach squeeze with excitement and nerves. I don't need that kind of distraction right now, especially after what I've seen. Getting romantically involved with Ryan will only make things more complicated. And harder, when it all goes to hell.

Zoe and I went for a run together on Sunday, and I filled her in on all the deets of the trip to see the sibyl. Well, almost all the deets. I didn't tell her about Melanie dying. And I didn't tell her about my vision. I'm not sure why I kept those two pieces from her. I normally told her everything. But she was getting deep enough in this that it was starting to involve her too. She knew Ryan. I didn't think she could regard his death as dispassionately as before. I didn't want to make it harder for her.

Zoe was, of course, thrilled at the prospect of a camping trip to Shasta. When the text came in from Ryan saying Brandon was in for the trip, her excited squeal practically blew my eardrums.

Ryan, Brandon, Zoe, and I set up a group text chain to prep for the trip. By some miracle, none of us have games or meets on Saturday, so we plan on leaving Friday night and returning Sunday. The drive is less than four hours one way, but we don't know how long it'll take us to find the entrance to the Byways or how long we'll need in Olympus. We want to give ourselves plenty of time.

Every time I see a text pop up from Ryan, I'm filled with giddy excitement—and, closely following on its heels, a sinking worry. I find myself missing Ryan and wanting to see him. I can't imagine the thought of him being gone for good. Never again seeing his rare but precious smile. The callouses on his palms. How he fills out his flannel shirt. I bury my face in my hands and let out a garbled cry. God, this sucks.

Brandon sidles up to me in history on Thursday and passes me a note. He looks around surreptitiously, to be sure no one is listening. No one is supposed to know that the four of us are camping together. Things in this school travel at the speed of light, and I can't risk something accidentally making its way back to my mom.

"What's this?" I ask, opening it.

"It's a suggested shopping list and meal plan for the trip," Brandon explains. "I'm open to suggestions, but I thought I'd get the ball rolling."

I scan it, my eyes opening wide. Breakfasts include: Pancakes, eggs, and bacon. Lunches are sandwiches with multiple meat and cheese options (havarti and pepper jack? Who is this guy?), and our two dinners will be burgers and fajitas. He even has snacks, beverages and desserts (s'mores, obvi) on here!

I look at him in disbelief. "Never, in all my years, have I encountered a member of the male species who actually plans ahead. This list might qualify as a genuine miracle."

He laughs. "We Cook men take camping extremely seriously. And there are two things that will make or break a camping trip. The food and the fire."

"I'm prepared to be astounded," I say as the teacher comes in and tells us to crack our books to page 148. We've graduated from the Spanish-American War and are now talking about the Industrial Revolution. "We'll take breakfast and lunch; you guys take dinner, snacks, and fire fixings?"

Brandon nods, his eyes bright. He's excited for this trip.

I force a smile, trying not to think about how this might be his last trip with his best friend.

The door opens and my mom appears, her red curls down around her shoulders. She crosses and speaks quickly with Mrs. Washburn, whose eyes slide to me. "Meriah?" she says. "You're needed in the office."

My face heats and I shove my stuff into my backpack. What the hell is Mom thinking, coming to summon me herself? I've done everything I can to distance us at school.

Brandon offers me a supportive smile as I walk up the row, the stares of my classmates burning into my back.

"What?" I round on Mom as soon as the door closes behind us.

She wraps her ivory cashmere cardigan around her like a shield. "Deputy Romano would like to speak with you again. He's in my office."

"Oh." My stomach sinks into the floor. "What about?"

"The accident, I would presume." Mom falls into step beside me, her heels clicking on the linoleum floor of the hallway. "You sure there's nothing else you remember?"

"Nothing," I offer, wracking my brain, thinking of all the

clues the deputy could have found to give us up. Our phones, the cabin, Ryan's camping story…

I'm not ready when my mom opens the door for me. She doesn't follow me in. I look over my shoulder, feeling exposed. I may not want her within ten feet of me most days at school, but she's still my mom. Her presence imparts a certain comfort.

"I asked your mom to wait outside. So we can talk alone." Deputy Romano smiles.

"Okay." I sink into the chair opposite him. "Do you have a lead on the hit-and-run driver?"

"We do," he says, the words chilling me to my core. "The lab found some paint fragments from the other car. They're from an ochre matte paint. It hasn't been made in about twenty-five years."

I blink, taking in his words. Twenty-five years. So he knows it's an old car. Like Ryan drives. And Ryan's truck is red. Or ochre, whatever the hell kind of color that is.

"There's also no record of Ryan staying at the campground he indicated. The camp host doesn't recall him."

I shrug. "There must be tons of people who come through those campgrounds."

"In April?" the deputy asks. "Not exactly high season."

"Why are you telling me this?"

"Meriah, we'll be getting a warrant to inspect Ryan's truck. If we find anything…it just seems odd that you were all the way out there. It's a far bike ride from town, especially at that time of night. It would make a lot more sense if you were riding with someone."

I realize what he means. He thinks I was in the car with Ryan.

He leans in, his face earnest. Concerned. Despite the threat he poses, I can't find myself disliking him. He's just doing his job. "Peer pressure is powerful. I wouldn't blame you if you were getting pressure from someone to stay quiet. But this is important. It's not your job to protect anyone. Okay?"

I nod, summoning my earnest face. "I was on my bike. I didn't even know who Ryan Kearney was that night. I swear." These things are true.

Deputy Romano searches my face. I don't know what he sees there, but I'm not going to cave. I'm not going to be the one who exposes Ryan. Finally, he stands. "Okay. Thanks."

I REPLAY my conversation with Deputy Romano about seventeen hundred times that day, and I keep reaching the same conclusion. There's not a damn thing I can do. We still need to break the curse. If anything, this weekend's trip is all the more urgent. I'm not sure what good will come of worrying everyone by telling them how close the police are to Ryan. Figuring a way to get Ryan out of Olympus alive feels like a far more pressing concern. So I swallow my worries and say nothing. Yet another secret I'm keeping from Zoe. It's an unfamiliar feeling, and one I don't like one bit.

Zoe and I drive to the store Thursday night to get our supplies for the trip. Zoe is the keeper of Brandon's list, which I think she's examined about thirty-eight times. I struggle to act normal. Everything's totally normal.

"I think you should ask him out," I tell Zoe as we pull into the Safeway parking lot.

"Ask him out?" she scoffs. "Are you insane?"

"What—it's not the 1800s anymore. Girls can ask guys out."

"But what if he says *no*? What if he just thinks of me as a friend and I totally humiliate myself?"

"That is a possibility—" I say jokingly, but at her pained

expression, I relent. "Zo—he's a good guy. If he's not interested, he'd just tell you that. He wouldn't be weird about it."

"How do you know?" she asks as we both get out of the car. I grab a lonely shopping cart that's been abandoned in the row, wheeling it towards the entrance. "Would a guy who could make a list like that be a dick about a girl liking him?" I point to said list.

She smiles. "No."

"Maybe he really likes you. Maybe you could be with him —but the only way you'll find out is asking. Isn't it worse not knowing?"

"No. Because not asking means I can continue to entertain my fantasies of him sweeping me off my feet with flowers and a prom invite."

I roll my eyes. "Nothing ventured, nothing gained, Zoe."

"I think the saying is, nothing ventured, nothing desperately crushed under the boot of one Brandon Cook."

We push through the automatic doors into the store. "I don't think that's how the saying goes—"

"Meriah?" a male voice says, and I snap to attention. It's Ryan Kearney, standing before me in all his teenage glory with a cart full of grocery bags. And sweet Jesus, his adorable grandma at his side.

"Hey, Ryan," I manage to respond.

Zoe waves.

"Doing a little grocery shopping?" Ryan asks innocently.

I push my lips together to keep a smile from my lips. This feels very illicit—the secret we share—that we're both shopping for our clandestine boy-girl camping trip.

"I guess Thursday's the night for it," I reply.

Ryan's grandma pushes forwards. I see a faint resemblance between them—the intense blue of their eyes, the shape of their noses. Even now, she's very pretty. "Is this the

Meriah I've been hearing so much about? I'm Ryan's grandmother, Eloise."

"Gran." Ryan's face flushes red, and I grin. I like her. I shake her offered hand.

"Yep. I'm Meriah, and this is my friend Zoe."

Zoe shakes too. "We go to school with Brandon," she says, as if explaining how we know Ryan. Though, really, it's just that Zoe's brain is made up of eight-five percent Brandon Cook.

"Very nice to meet you both." Eloise smiles at us, and I see similarities in their smile, too. My heart twists painfully. "Ryan's lucky to have a good friend like Brandon." She pats him on his shoulder.

"I think they're lucky to have each other," I say, and Ryan's face softens at my words.

"Well, we've got milk to get in the fridge." Ryan's grandmother gracefully excuses them from this strangest of conversations. "Nice to meet you both."

"Nice to meet you too," Zoe and I say in chorus. I give Ryan a wave, letting my eyes drink in the sight of him. "See you later." Though *see you tomorrow* would be far more accurate. Tomorrow, when we undertake a foolishly dangerous mission that will likely lead to your death.

"She's so cute," Zoe whispers to me as we head into the bread aisle. "I hope I'm that cute when I'm old."

"Are you kidding? Your grandma is adorable. You will totes be that cute," I manage to reply, though my thoughts are mired in the mud of Ryan Kearney.

"Do you think we'll still be friends when we're old ladies?" Zoe asks.

"Without a doubt." I give Zoe a sideways squeeze, and it seems to mollify her. She pulls out the list and takes charge, leaving me to push the cart. Somehow, it's made it worse, meeting Ryan's grandmother. Seeing how she regards him so fondly, her weathered hand lingering on his shoulder. He's clearly her world, and by keeping secrets—Deputy Romano's suspicions, my vision—I'm going to take that world away. I'd always thought Orion was the monster in my story—Orion and Zeus. But now I'm not so sure. Maybe all along, the monster has been me.

CHAPTER 26

We're all crowded into Brandon's SUV, our camping gear piled to the ceiling behind us. We're only supposed to be gone for two nights, but it seems like we brought enough stuff for a week. Half of the back is filled with firewood. When Zoe and I suggested it might be overkill, Brandon and Ryan looked so outraged that we backed off. What is it with boys and fire?

Zoe and I met the guys in the Walmart parking lot, where we transferred our gear and left Zoe's car. We couldn't exactly have loaded our stuff directly into their car—not with our parents thinking this was strictly a Mer-Zo camping trip.

The day is bright and blue, and Ryan has found the 'Road Trip' mix on his Spotify app and is blasting it through the car's speakers. Brandon is drumming the steering wheel and singing along, his voice unabashedly out of tune. Nice to find something the guy's not perfect at. I should be feeling on top of the world. I love road trips—there's something about the wind and the sun and the road that makes me feel so *free*. I love camping. I love Zoe. I…like…Ryan. My mind trips over the words. We're headed to break the curse. This should be the best frickin' day in my entire life. Yet I can't untie the heavy knot in the pit of my stomach. Or banish the memory of Ryan's booted feet sticking out from behind that pillar. Even if we are successful at breaking the curse, this trip will very likely end in tragedy. My mind flashes to the ride back…with just three of us. And even if I find some miraculous way to break the curse and save Ryan, what's waiting for him? Deputy Romano's face surfaces, his words echoing in my mind. *A warrant to inspect Ryan's truck.* How long does it take to get a warrant?

I look out the window, glad my sunglasses shade the tears pooling in the corners of my eyes. The Fates have dropped me smackdab in the middle of a rock and a hard place. And I don't have the first clue what to do.

I feel a poke in my side, and I turn. Zoe is raising an eyebrow at me in a what-the-hell-is-up-with-you look. I can't keep secrets from her. She knows me too well.

I force a smile and give her the thumbs up. She scrunches her lips suspiciously, and I can tell that this is not over.

"I have a proposal." Brandon looks at us through the rearview mirror. He's wearing silver-mirrored aviators and a form-fitting T-shirt and I must say is looking pretty fine. How Zoe is keeping her cool right now is beyond me.

"Do tell," Zoe replies.

"We each share our most hilarious camping story—and whoever gets the least laughs has to cook dinner."

Ryan looks back with a crooked grin. "I thought the girls were handling dinner."

"What a sexist thing to suggest, Mr. Kearney," I say with outrage that is only half-faked. "I'll have you know Zoe and I excel at all sorts of traditionally male tasks."

"You *are* excellent kidnappers, which I do think of as a traditionally male task," Ryan deadpans.

Brandon explodes in laughter in the driver's seat, putting his fist out to give Ryan a fist bump.

"Har har," I say. "Fine, Brandon, we'll play. But, Ryan, I like my burgers medium well, all right? It's important to get the consistency right."

"Hope you build that fire right, then," he shoots back. "It's all about the even flame distribution."

"Okay," Brandon interjects. "Who wants to go first?"

"I will." Zoe launches into a story about backpacking with her brother that I've heard before. "So this couple is coming up the mountain, and you can just tell they're furious. They have this big white poodle trotting beside them—but it's got this big ol' smear of brown on its back. And the guy is just livid—he looks straight at Jason and me as we pass them, saying 'our dog rolled in shit back there!' And in his high-pitched voice, he goes, 'And I think it was human shit!' And we're all sympathetic, like, 'Who would do something like that…?' but the second they get out of sight we look at each other and realize that the couple just passed the spot where Jason had, you know, done his business on the way up the trail."

Ryan and Brandon are howling in the front. Leave it to a poop or fart story to bring a guy to tears. "So let me get this straight." Brandon wipes the corner of his eyes. "The dog rolled in your brother's shit, and then the people were complaining to you about it?"

"Yep." Zoe nods, laughing.

Even though I've heard the story before, I'm still busting up. It feels good to laugh out loud, to release that tension.

Ryan's phone rings and the sound resounds through the car. It's hooked into the Bluetooth. "It's Gran. Mind if I take it?"

"You do you, bro," Brandon says.

Ryan looks over his shoulder at us and holds up a finger

for silence. Zoe feigns zipping her lips. Ryan doesn't want to have to explain to dear old grandma why there are female voices in the background.

Ryan hits the green button. "Hey, Gran. What's up?"

"Ryan, where are you?" Gran's shaky voice fills the car. She sounds distraught.

Ryan and Brandon exchange a look of alarm. "On the road."

"You need to come home right now."

"What?" Ryan sits up. "What happened?"

"Oh, Ryan." She's almost in tears. I realize what's happened a split second before she says it. "There's a sheriff's deputy here. He has a warrant to search your truck."

Silence falls over the car, thick and cloying as wet wool.

"What?" Ryan manages.

"They think you hit some poor girl. It's a misunderstanding, I know it. Just get home right away."

I can see Ryan's jaw working, his fingers curling around his knees. "The keys are in my room. Let them take what they need. And I'm sorry, but I can't come home yet. There's something I have to do first."

"Ryan—" she starts, but he punches the red button and the call drops out. The music resumes, a crowing acoustic rendition of *Free Fallin'*. And that's just how I feel. Like my life is pinwheeling into empty air.

"Do you want to go back?" Brandon asks quietly.

Ryan shakes his head, his face stony. "This is my only shot at this. We keep going."

PANTHER MEADOW CAMPGROUND is the closest campground to the slopes of Mount Shasta, located at almost eight thousand feet of elevation. The sun is setting by the time we arrive, sending streaks of orange slanting through the tall firs. Though the campground is "walk in," the path from the parking lot to the campsites isn't too long. Half an hour later, we've schlepped all our stuff from the car and Ryan's working on the fire while Brandon and Zoe manhandle together the huge tent Brandon brought. It feels good to be doing something—to replace the tense silence that permeated the rest of the drive. Apparently, we've all independently decided to pretend there isn't a sheriff's deputy searching Ryan's vehicle as we speak. It's fine by me. 'Cause I don't know what the hell to say.

"It's like camping with the King of Sheba." I nod over my shoulder at the red nylon monstrosity as I pull food out of the cooler.

"I think Brandon's family are like founding REI members," Ryan says. "They like their gear fancy and expensive."

"Must be nice," I mutter. My family has money, but my parents have still always bought my gear on clearance or secondhand. They always said I grew out of it too fast to spend a fortune on it.

"Yes, it is," Ryan agrees.

I'm rearranging various items under the picnic table to put them out of the way when I come across two large rectangular cases. "What are these?"

"My bows."

"You brought two?"

"Sibyll said we'd be facing off against boobytraps and stuff in there. I thought it would be good to be armed."

"But why two?"

"One for Brandon." Ryan blows on his little teepee of kindling and little flames whoosh to life.

I've been thinking about whether Brandon and Zoe will

go into Olympus with us, and I have to say, I don't like it. I lower my voice. "I don't want them going in with us."

Ryan looks up from the fire.

I crouch down, keeping my voice quiet. "It's not their fight. I could never forgive myself if something happened to one of them in there. You and I will be reincarnated, but them? I think we should leave them behind."

"They'll never agree to stay behind," Ryan protests. "I know Brandon. He won't take *no* for an answer."

"So we don't let them know they're staying behind. Until it's too late."

Ryan rubs his jaw, considering. And then he nods. "Agreed."

Relief floods me. The thought of anything happening to Zoe had me wrapped in knots.

"Maybe I should take the other bow."

Ryan blinks at me, pinning me with those ocean-blue eyes. "Meriah, this isn't a sexist comment or anything, but I don't know if you could shoot the bow. They're challenging, and it takes a lot of upper body strength. The draw weight on these two bows is designed for a man. If I was going to start you out, I'd pick something lighter. "

I prickle. "There's only one way to find out."

"What do you mean?" He looks at me, suddenly on guard.

"Show me how to shoot it."

"Mer…"

"Or are you not a good enough teacher?" I challenge him.

"It's not about teaching." He growls in frustration. "Fine." He stretches to his feet, all lean and tall. He's in green Carhartt pants, work boots, and a black T-shirt. He's got a Cabela's camo hat on. I'm not big into the hunter redneck look, but Ryan makes it look good.

He starts off through the forest, and I call after him. "Where are you going?"

"Going to make sure we don't kill anyone," he hollers back.

Oh. That's smart.

A few minutes later Ryan tromps back through the trees. I guess the coast is clear. He hauls up one of the cases onto the table and unzips it. The compound bow inside is a complex killing device, all angles and wheels and strings. With it in his hand, he transforms from Ryan Kearney to something different. Older. It's like I'm seeing double vision. This is Ryan—and Orion. He hands it to me and the vision clears. I shake off my unease.

The bow is heavy in my hands. Much heavier than I thought. Suddenly, this seems like a bad idea.

"Tell me what you do when you draw it."

He sighs. He reaches around me and holds the bow steady while his other hand tilts my hand into position. He begins instructing me. Legs hip-distance apart, knees straight but easy. Shoulders angled slightly. Hand on grip at forty-five-degree angle, in contact with the fleshy part of the palm. Arrow resting in the arrow rest, wrist through a little loop that draws back the string. He smells of hay and pine needles and the glittering expanse of the night sky. I'm finding it hard to focus on the task before me with the heat of his body radiating into mine.

"Maybe I should just try pulling the string without an arrow," I say, suddenly unsure.

"It's not a good idea. We don't want to risk dry firing the bow. It can damage it." Ryan connects the little loop around my wrist to the back of the string. Everything is different than I expected. Automated. I don't hold the arrow. I don't even use my fingers to pull back the string. "Okay, now pull in a smooth motion, back towards your jaw," he says. A knife is sounding preferable, but I'm too proud to admit I'm wrong.

I pull, and nothing happens. The force against me is strong. I pull again, summoning every bit of strength in my arm. The bowstring moves into position.

I let out a little squeal of delight.

"Good job," Ryan says gruffly, taking my shoulders and angling me gently towards the tree we have decided is our target. Out of the corner of my eye, I can see that Zoe and Brandon have finished setting up the tent and are watching.

"Now wrap your finger around the trigger, and when you're ready, release."

I breathe out, then pull the trigger. The arrow explodes from the bow and buries itself in the tree. I can't believe it!

I turn to Ryan in disbelief. "I hit it!" He *whoops* and pulls me into a hug, swinging me around. I bury my face in the crook of his shoulder, never wanting to let go.

My feet touch the ground again, and he pulls back. His eyes are bright and seem to trace the contours of my face, my lips. I'm hyperaware of where his hand lingers on my hip. Mine lingers on his shoulder. Damn it, I want to kiss him.

Zoe and Brandon are clapping and cheering in the background, which shakes me out of my Ryan-induced daze.

"You're a natural," Ryan says. "Want to try again?"

"Hell no!" I hand the bow back to him like it's a rattlesnake. I know it took all of my strength to pull that string once. I don't think I could do it again.

Just like it will take all my strength to face whatever tomorrow brings.

CHAPTER 27

My mood grows darker as night falls, and not even s'mores are enough to cheer me up. I don't want Ryan to die. The feel of his arms around me is burned into my memory, like brands on my skin. I've kissed two boys before—Billy McGregor in seventh grade, and my freshman crush, Adam Kowalski—and my memory of kissing either of them doesn't even hold a candle to how alive I feel when Ryan is near.

I have a horrible thought. What if we're soulmates and we were supposed to find each other in all of these lives, but my prejudices and distrust of him got in the way? I could have had fifty happy lifetimes...but instead... No. I reject the notion. The Fates wouldn't be that kind. Even if Ryan is my soulmate, the Fates would have set us up to go down in a blaze of glory, Romeo and Juliet style, every lifetime. Probably all I missed out on was heartbreak.

Besides, I'm not even sure I believe in soulmates. Though reincarnate a girl enough times, and she might believe in just about anything.

I adjust in my sleeping bag, huffing, trying to get

comfortable. There's a pointy rock under me, which feels like the perfect metaphor for my life. We had a delish dinner that, despite the guys' big talk, we all pitched in on, and then we sat around Ryan and Brandon's bonfire talking until our toes and faces grew too warm and we had to move back. As much as I harped on the guys to conserve wood for a morning fire, I think they used most of it up. No one mentioned the call from Ryan's grandma or the uncertain fate that awaits us tomorrow. It felt so much better to embrace the role of care-free teenager on illicit co-ed camping trip with swoonworthy crush.

"Mer," Zoe whispers, turning in her sleeping bag to face me. Her cherubic face peeking out of her blue mummy bag is the only part of her I can see.

"What?"

"What's up with you? You were quiet all night. Now you're tossing and turning like a bucking bronco. Are you just worried about Deputy Romano or is it something else? You okay?"

I close my eyes briefly. No, I am not okay. I turn back to look over my shoulder to where Ryan and Brandon are sleeping a few feet away. Seriously, you could fit a small house inside this tent Brandon brought. They're both asleep, their breathing even. If I don't tell someone, I think I might explode. I turn back and keep my voice low. "You know how Alcyone almost died in Corvallis? And I thought we'd foiled the curse?"

"Yeah…"

I shake my head, burying my face in the nylon of my sleeping bag for a moment. "I saw on the news later that night. She died suddenly."

"Oh Mer—" Zoe begins, but Ryan interrupts her. "What?" He's sitting straight up in his sleeping bag, his eyes gleaming balefully at me in the dark.

"Do you have like Superman hearing?" I ask in annoyance. Damn it. He wasn't supposed to know. This will only make things worse.

Brandon stirs beside him. "Keep it down," he mumbles. "Sleepytime."

Ryan unzips his sleeping bag and gets out, stepping into his boots. He's wearing red flannel pajama pants, a black hoodie, and a gray beanie. I wish I could tell you I'm focused enough to ignore how cute he looks in his pajamas. But alas, I am not that girl.

I unzip my sleeping bag as well, shivering as the cold air hits me. The temperature dropped significantly as soon as the sun went down. It's only April, after all, and we're at eight thousand feet. I slip my feet into my UGGs, grab my puffy jacket, and follow Ryan out into the night. The stars are a tapestry above us, the stretch of Orion dominating the velvet sky. He's always been there, hasn't he? Close enough to touch, yet impossibly distant. A fixture in my many lives that I've only just come to realize the importance of. Right when I'm going to lose him.

Ryan rounds on me when we reach the dark fire pit, his hands shoved in the pockets of his hoodie. My breath puffs before me like smoke, my nose tickling from the cold.

"So she died?" he asks. The heartbreak written on his face hits me like a punch to the gut. "I thought… How did you…?"

"I saw it on the news," I say. "That night. I couldn't sleep; my parents had it on. Some sort of complication."

"And you kept this from me why?"

"I…didn't want you to feel bad," I say lamely. The truth is, as soon as I had the vision of his still body, I pulled away from him. Because our budding alliance was wrecked. Once again I was the faithless girl who was going to sacrifice him for the good of her sisters.

A shiver wracks me, and he steps close, rubbing his hands

up and down my arms. "You're freezing. You should get back in your sleeping bag."

But neither of us moves. His hands slow and he pulls me into his chest, wrapping his arms around me.

I lean into his warmth, resting my head on the hard plane of his chest, squeezing my eyes closed. His heart is hammering a staccato beat beneath my ear. "You don't have to bear it all alone, Mer," he murmurs into my hair, and it breaks me. Because I've been bearing this burden alone for so many lifetimes, I don't even know what the alternative would look like. A sob escapes my mouth and his arms tighten around me. I breathe in his campfire smells of woodsmoke and caramelized sugar, trying to center myself. It doesn't work, and more tears fall, wetting his sweatshirt.

"Hey, it's okay." He pulls back slightly, searching my face with his eyes. He raises one hand and cups my cheek, his thumb brushing across the trail of my tears. As if one touch from him is enough to erase them all.

I look up at him and forget everything but Ryan. The landscape of his face, the secret curve of his lips, the endless blue of his eyes. A flush across my skin banishes the cold as he tilts his head and brings his mouth down to mine. His lips are firm yet soft and move with practiced ease. I press myself closer to him and part my lips, letting his tongue caress my own.

I wish I could tell you that kissing Ryan is like molten heat mixed with effervescent joy. Because it is. But all I can taste is my guilt. I'm leading Ryan to his death. And what's worse, I've been lying about it.

Another tear slides down my face, the salt mingling with the sweetness of our kiss. Ryan breaks off gently, leaning his forehead against mine and drawing in a breath. "I hope you're not crying over how bad my kissing is." He chuckles huskily.

I push away from him, turning my back to him, burying my face in my icy fingers.

"Mer?" he asks, uncertain. "I'm sorry. If that wasn't what you wanted—"

I whirl around, words bubbling forth. "There's something else. That I didn't tell you." I can no more hold in the truth than I can halt the tears now flowing freely down my face.

He takes a step towards me, suddenly wary. His hands go back into his pockets. "What?"

I look down, grateful for the dark. "I had another vision."

"Who?" is all he asks. He knows what I mean.

I look up and see he's bracing himself for a blow.

"You."

Ryan recoils, taking a step back. "Me?"

I nod, misery flooding me. "It was in a sort of throne room. Roman columns. I think…" I can't say it.

"I die in there." His tone is flat. No nonsense.

I nod again, trying to read his face, but it's turned in shadow.

"And when were you going to tell me?"

I swallow.

"Ah. I see. You weren't. This was your plan along? You had no problem releasing me because you knew the Fates would take care of me soon enough."

"No." I shake my head violently. "I didn't know then. I only had the vision after we got back from seeing the sibyl."

I'm not sure he heard me. He steps towards me, nervous energy radiating off him. I hold my ground. "You were leading me like a lamb to the slaughter this whole time, weren't you? I thought we were partners in this, but all along, I was your sacrifice to the gods."

"That's not true—" I protest.

He cuts in harshly. "Nothing matters to you but your

sisters, does it? Breaking this stupid curse. I don't matter at all to you."

"That's not true, Ryan," I plead, desperate for him to believe me. To see how this is shattering me into pieces smaller than I thought possible. "You're all I think about. If there was any other way…"

"But you didn't even look for another way, did you? Sacrificing me was an acceptable cost to you. God, I was such an idiot!"

He turns and starts off into the dark forest.

"Where are you going?" I screech.

"Anywhere away from you," he throws over his shoulder.

And then he's gone, swallowed into the darkness of the night. Leaving me alone in the dark, with nothing but tingling lips and a shattered heart.

CHAPTER 28

I don't get a wink of sleep that night. I burrow into my sleeping bag, ignoring Brandon's and Zoe's murmured questions upon my return. I squeeze closed even the little face hole until I'm completely cocooned in down, hidden from the world. In this warm little world, I let my tears fall freely, the drops drawing little trails into my ears. It's as close as I can get to being swallowed up by the ground, which is what I'd really like right now. I can't believe it. Ryan kissed me. And then I ruined everything.

At some point I hear the tent flap open, and I know Ryan must have returned. I'm glad—it was making me feel even more miserable to imagine him out there shivering in the night. I don't breach my sleeping bag fortress to look at him, though I want to. I can't face him right now. Maybe ever again.

My body is stiff and grumpy when the sky above the tent starts to lighten, signaling dawn. My mind is miserable, still churning with thoughts and worries, running down alternative paths like bunnies down a rabbit hole. And my heart— I'm not sure it will ever be the same.

One of the guys stirs, getting out of his sleeping bag. I peek and see it's Ryan. I'm not surprised. I doubt he got much sleep, either.

I hear rustling by the fire pit, followed by the low crackling of kindling lighting.

Brandon gets up next, then Zoe and me. By the time the two of us return from the pit toilet a few hundred yards up the trail, the fire is going, and Brandon is pulling bacon out of the cooler.

"Bacon." Zoe smiles happily at Brandon, and he grins back. "And coffee," he adds. He shakes a little pocket of Starbucks instant in her direction.

"I've never seen a more beautiful sight." She sighs, and Brandon chuckles. I wonder if he realizes she's talking about him, not the coffee.

Zoe and Brandon's exchange stirs the pieces of my shattered heart like leaves in a breeze. Just yesterday, Ryan looked at me like that. Now he won't look at me at all.

The guys cook the bacon on foil over the fire while Zoe and I scramble some eggs and boil water for the coffee on the camp stove.

"Are you okay?" she whispers to me. "What happened last night?"

I just shake my head, fighting back tears. "I don't want to talk about it."

She understands and gives me a side hug. I welcome the comfort. At least I'll always have Zoe. A best friend has salved many a broken heart.

Brandon *whoops* as the grease from the bacon slides into the fire, causing a jet of flame to scoot skywards. "Hope you girls like it well done!"

Zoe laughs, and a ghost of a smile meets my lips. As shitty as this day may be, at least there's coffee and bacon.

When breakfast is ready, we sit down in our chairs

around the fire to eat and Ryan clears his throat. My head whips up, my senses trilling to high alert. I don't know what's going to happen now that I've told Ryan what awaits him in Olympus. I don't blame him if he packs up and gets the hell out of here. Though the reception waiting for him at home… is not exactly friendly.

"Meriah told me something last night that I think you both should know," he says, talking to Brandon and Zoe. He still hasn't looked at me. I'm amazed he's even using my name. I half expected to be addressed as "she who shall not be named."

Brandon rests his fork, perking up. His curls are even more tousled this morning, giving him this soft adorable look. Zoe must be dying.

"Meriah had a vision of Olympus."

Zoe's head whips my way, her expression hurt. She's always first to hear about my visions.

Ryan continues. "Apparently, I…don't make it back."

Silence falls over the circle. A log in the fire pops, and we all jump at the sudden rain of sparks.

"I thought about it a lot last night, and it doesn't change anything. I'm still going," Ryan says.

My mouth goes dry. He's going to walk into Olympus, even knowing what it means? I close my eyes. Damn it, why does he have to be so honorable? I realize now that I wanted him to run. It's why I told him. I wanted him to be selfish and do everything he could to preserve his life. Because then I could keep him in this lifetime. He might not be mine, and I'd have to hate him for endangering the rest of my sisters, but at least he'd still be here. And I wouldn't have been the one to make the selfish choice.

"Are you insane?" Brandon asks. "It's one thing walking into a super dangerous magical boobytrapped lair of the gods with only your bow to defend you, but to go in *knowing* you're not going to come out? What are you trying to prove?"

"I'm not trying to prove anything," Ryan says. "Two of Mer's sisters have already died in this lifetime because of me. There are four left. If I do this, if we end the curse, I save them. One life for four. When you do the math, there's no question."

Brandon glances at me, like he's weighing what he wants to say in front of me. "No offense, Mer, but I don't know those girls. I do know you, man. You're...my brother. You can't just, like...sacrifice yourself."

Ryan's voice catches as he responds. "It's not like I'm going to go in with a target on my chest and let them kill me. We'll fight. All of us. Maybe we can beat it. Break the curse *and* come out of there alive."

"Has one of Meriah's visions ever not come true?" Brandon looks at me.

My silence says all it needs to. Though Alcyone didn't die how I saw it in my vision, in the end, she died all the same.

"This isn't easy for me, either, Brandon." Ryan's voice is soft. "But I've decided."

Brandon pushes to his feet, the rest of his breakfast forgotten. His face is blotchy. "I need a minute."

Ryan stands to follow as if he's unsure, but then sits back down.

Zoe's looking with me with such sympathy that I almost break down again.

"Can I talk to you alone for a minute?" I ask Ryan. I need to explain to him how hard this decision was for me. How I didn't want to sacrifice him. What his decision means to me. Some bit of the tornado of emotions spinning inside me.

"I've heard all I need to from you," Ryan replies icily. "Let's just get ready to go."

~

Mount Shasta is breathtaking against the azure sky. Our boots trudge down a packed dirt trail that winds through emerald green meadows sprinkled with wildflowers and stands of weathered pines and firs. It's a beautiful day for a hike—but it feels more like a death march. I guess it is, for one of us. Ryan walks in front, Sibyll's key in his hand, leading our way. We don't know how far we have to hike to the door to the Byway, but I hope it's not long. The tense silence stretched between us makes me want to scream.

An hour in, the key swings wildly in Ryan's hand, drawing us off the main path, up a hillside covered in purple larkspur and yellow poppies. The sun has banished the morning's chill and sweat beads my brow. Ryan and Brandon carry the two bows, and Zoe and I each have knife holsters threaded into our belts, reminding me inexorably that this is no simple day hike.

As we climb, a cluster of gray granite boulders appears above us to the right. As soon as I see them, a knowing trills in me. This is the place. The doorway. Part of me is surprised we found it so easily. But I know what waits for us on the other side will not be so simple.

"That's it." Ryan quickens his pace.

Zoe looks at me with a raised eyebrow and I nod.

I heave a breath as I reach the outcropping, taking a sip of water from my CamelBak. This close, I can feel the vibration of the rocks, a buzzing that puts my teeth on edge.

"This is it all right," I agree.

Ryan turns to us, looking at Zoe and Brandon, again his gaze sliding over me. "We stick together in there, okay? No one plays the hero."

"You especially," Brandon says.

Ryan finally meets my eyes, and I give a curt nod. If

there's one thing that Ryan and I are still united on, it's the fact that Brandon and Zoe will not be going to Olympus with us. We won't risk them. Too many people have died already.

We thread our hands together—Zoe, me, Ryan, Brandon. Ryan's hand is limp in my grip, as if he can hardly stomach my touch. In that moment, I long for any sign that the Ryan I fell for is still in there, even a reassuring squeeze. I get one from Zoe, and I give her a halfhearted smile. Damn it, is there no one I'm not going to betray today?

The four of us turn to the rock grotto before us and step forwards. The hairs on the back of my neck raise; I can feel that magic is close. Another step and we'll be through whatever barrier separates our world from the Byway.

"Now," Ryan says, and we both release our grips on our other friends, jumping forwards. The key in Ryan's pocket carries us through the magical barrier, but Zoe and Brandon bump against an invisible wall and stumble back, Zoe falling to one knee.

"What the hell?" Brandon protests, helping Zoe up.

She sees what's going on right away. My girl is too smart for her own good. "Mer, don't do this," Zoe protests.

"This isn't your fight," I croak. "I can't lose you too."

"Ryan, no." Brandon bangs a fist against the invisible wall that now stands between us. "I'll have your back in there. I can help!"

Ryan drops my hand. "Take care of Gran for me, okay?"

"Ryan—don't—"

"I love you, Brandon," Ryan says. "I was lucky to have a brother like you."

Then he turns and we step through the doorway that's appeared in the rock before us, the sounds of our friends' cries chasing in our wake.

CHAPTER 29

The world closes around us as we step through the doorway into the Byway. I'm not sure what I imagined, but it wasn't this. It's pitch black here and as silent as death, but for Ryan and my ragged breathing. "I have my headlamp," I say, unshouldering my pack and kneeling down, fumbling into the depths. I've never experienced such an absence of light. Not even in the space between lifetimes.

My fingers close around the strap of my headlamp and I sigh audibly in relief. I switch it on and stand, adjusting it on my head. It doesn't illuminate much. Mist shrouds us, obscuring all but a stone path beneath our feet. In my unease I slip my fingers into his, but he immediately lets go of my hand. "Let's go."

The key tugs Ryan's hand forwards, but it seems there's only one way to go, at least for the time being. My unease over this place is punctured by my misery over leaving Zoe and Brandon. It was the right call, but still, the look of betrayal on their faces haunts me. The thought of coming back to face them without Ryan by my side...I don't know if I can do it.

168

"Ryan," I say quietly as the mist seems to swallow the word.

"Not now," he replies. "We said what we needed to say. We need to focus."

"I didn't say what I needed to," I protest.

He heaves a long-suffering sigh. "Fine. Talk."

But I'm tongue-tied. I search for the words to explain the confusion that swirls within me. "I don't want you to die," is all that comes out.

He snorts. "I suppose that's something."

"That kiss—"

He cuts me off sharply. "Forget the kiss. It was a bad idea."

"No, it wasn't." I summon my courage. "I wanted you to kiss me. I still do."

He looks at me in the dark, my headlamp shining garishly on his face. "Throwing me under the bus is a funny way of showing it."

"What was I supposed to do? Whatever happens with you or me, we have this one shot to break the curse. We've never been this close in any other lifetime. I'd give anything to end it. Even you. Or…me." I realize it's true. I would give my life if it meant bringing all this to a close. Sure, it would be nice to live one curse-free happy lifetime, but hadn't I had way more lives than a person is entitled to, even if she's half-Titan?

"You don't get it, do you?"

"Enlighten me."

"It's not that you think my life is a fair trade to end the curse. Obviously, I do too; otherwise, I wouldn't be here. It's that you didn't tell me. You didn't think enough of me to think I would do the right thing."

I straighten, surprised. I guess I didn't get it. That was not on my list of possibilities for why he was mad.

Ryan shakes his head.

"We're still getting to know each other," I protest weakly. "I thought you were my enemy for lifetimes. I'm still... learning to trust you. And it wasn't that I didn't think you'd do the right thing. I didn't want to put that burden on you. Knowing the time and manner of your own death is a pretty shitty thing. I learned that the hard way in the early lifetimes, when I tried to save my sisters by telling them. At some point, it just becomes a self-fulfilling prophecy."

He's pondering that when the key swings wildly to the left, almost into me. We stop and I turn, letting my light illuminate the darkness before us.

"There." I point. My light is shining on a stone wall a few yards off the path.

We approach, and the wall sharpens into focus. There's a door etched into its surface, flanked by two carved Grecian columns. A keyhole peers at us quietly.

"Looks like we're here." I let out a nervous laugh.

He puts the key into the keyhole and turns. The door swings inward, revealing a dark tile floor and a room beyond.

"Ready?" Ryan asks.

"Does it matter?"

Ryan takes my hand, threading his fingers through mine, and it gives me all the certainty I need. We step through.

The room is still and quiet. My footsteps stir a thick layer of dust on the marble beneath our feet, and I sneeze.

Ryan retrieves the key and puts it in his pocket, closing the door behind us. We didn't encounter anything in the Byway, but that doesn't mean there isn't anything out there.

"Think the key will show us where the scythe is?" I joke. I don't like how quiet or still it is here. It feels like the moment in a horror movie before something horrible jumps out at you.

"I don't think we'll be so lucky."

"Zeus used to keep the scythe in his throne room. I guess we should try there first?"

"As good a theory as any," Ryan agrees. He drops my hand, but it doesn't feel as hostile as last time. He unshoulders his bow, getting it into position. "Any idea which direction that is?"

"None at all." I take out my knife, feeling like it's going to be seriously inferior to whatever task it encounters in here. I thought about asking Brandon for the other bow, but who are we kidding? I'd be better off thwacking a monster with it than actually trying to draw it again in the heat of battle.

"Let's head that way," Ryan says, nodding straight ahead of us. "I have some memories of the palace at Olympus. If I can figure out where we are, I should be able to navigate us there."

We soldier forwards, our hiking boots leaving trails in the undisturbed dust. How many centuries has it been since someone visited here? The sibyl's warning rings in my mind. Olympus will be guarded. But if there've been any monsters prowling here lately, they're the incorporeal kind. At the door into a hallway, I spot a darkened torch in a sconce on the wall.

"Lighter?" I ask.

Ryan turns his back to me so I can fish it out of his pack. I light the torch and the cheerful blaze comforts me. It's easier to see by the light of the torch so I turn my headlamp off, leaving it hanging around my neck.

"Lead the way."

Our slow sojourn down the hallway brings memories bubbling up. The hallway is lined with ornate alcoves sporting tall marble statues of mythical creatures. A centaur, the three-headed dog Cerberus, who guards the underworld. A strange gryphon with the head and wings of an eagle and the body of a lion. The Greek gods sure loved to mix and match; they treated the whole animal kingdom like a bestial Mr. Potato Head. The arched ceiling above us is painted with clouds and blue sky, not that anyone would be fooled to think they're outside. "I think I remember this corridor," I say as we near the end. "Go right. If I'm right, there should be a—

"Fountain of Poseidon," Ryan finishes as we enter the room. The carved fountain looms before us, its leaping dolphins dark and silent. The fountain is dry, but I'm not surprised. Water means life, and there's no life here. Not anymore.

Now that Ryan and I know where we are, we walk more quickly. We pass through the long room that was once filled with diners both mortal and immortal, and all the delicacies Olympus had to offer. The long, polished wood tables stand empty and quiet, flanked by rows of chairs facing off like soldiers. We leave them behind, walking through the octagonal antechamber into Zeus's throne room.

My heart is in my throat as I hold the torch aloft, my eyes searching the inlaid walls of the cavernous space for the item we seek. The scythe of Chronos.

"Holy hell, it's here!" A disbelieving laugh escapes Ryan's lips.

I want to weep with relief. For there—hanging on its hooks behind the marble hulk of Zeus's empty throne—is the scythe. Just where my sister once retrieved it.

The blood of my sisters is gone from the polished floor, but I can't help but feel the poignancy of the moment. "This is where it all started," I say, my eyes affixed to the scythe.

"It's fitting that this is where it ends," Ryan agrees.

"I have to admit, after what Sibyll said, I thought it'd be harder to find," I muse.

Ryan huffs. "Find some wood to knock on, why don't

you? We haven't broken the curse yet. Do you have any idea how to wield that thing? To end the curse?"

"None whatsoever," I admit.

Great, he mouths with a shake of his head.

"How are we going to get it down?" I ask. It's nestled atop two hooks on the wall.

Ryan draws his bow, aims, and looses an arrow. It buries itself into the wall, busting off one of the hooks. The scythe tips out of the other hook and tumbles to the floor with a clatter.

It's my turn to huff. "Hope it's not breakable."

I step forwards to retrieve the weapon. And the ground starts to shake.

CHAPTER 30

The scythe is heavy in my hand, but I fear it won't be substantial enough to face whatever's coming. Because the shaking has transformed into the thunder of pounding feet. "What should we do?" I ask, my brain refusing to cooperate with our current predicament.

"Get the hell out of here." Ryan nods his head towards the exit to the throne room.

"We haven't broken the curse yet," I protest.

"We don't know how to break the curse," he says. "And I'm not inclined to just hand myself over on a silver platter while you sit around trying to figure it out."

Oh gods, the vision. Ryan's boots peeking out from behind the column. The thick blood congealed around him. His vacant eyes…

"Let's go," I agree. We break into a run, our boots pounding against the polished floor. We skid into the hallway, and my heart leaps into my throat. They've found us. The defenders of this place. And they're coming right at us.

"Retreat!" Ryan screams and we scramble back into the throne room, dashing for a doorway behind the raised dais.

My mind still struggles to make sense of what it's seen. Statues come to life. The stone menagerie we passed has come alive and is now set upon our destruction. The stone leopard bursts through the doorway at the far end of the throne room with a snarl.

I risk a glance over my shoulder. Its passage has ripped chunks of stone from beside the opening, spraying them in a deadly hail of rock projectiles. The other creatures are hot on its heels—I see the three-headed dog, a gryphon, and a centaur. The centaur aims its bow at us and I screech and duck. The stone arrow buries itself in the wall just inches from my head.

But there's no time for marveling or wondering or even thinking. There's only time for running. We barrel through an antechamber into a circular room with an arched ceiling that must have been Zeus's treasure trove. All around us objects glitter—the vast wealth of Olympus. I'd give my left arm for a few moments to linger over the items—priceless statues, delicate gem-encrusted jewelry, intricately painted pottery.

"My bow," Ryan breathes, skidding to a stop as we reach the far end of the room.

I can hear the creatures' hooves and claws scratching and sliding on the slick floor of the antechamber. They're close.

Ryan drops his compound bow and grabs his ancient one —shouldering the brightly-painted quiver. I spot a glittering shield hanging on the wall and grab it, threading my forearm through the leather straps.

The bow looks right in his hands, transforming him into the hunter I remember from Merope's memories. "Think they can be killed?" he asks, notching an arrow.

"I sure as hell hope so," I say as the leopard appears in the doorway, snarling and baring its wicked stone teeth. It's fixated upon us, its tail swishing. "'Cause we sure can."

Ryan looses an arrow. The shaft flies straight and true, burying itself in the leopard's eye.

The big cat screeches with pain and charges at us.

"Run!" I'm not sure if it's me or Ryan who says it.

We're on the move again, pounding down a long, dark hallway. I try not to think about how many arrows it will take to bring that thing down. At least it didn't just ricochet off the creature's stone skin. That's something.

The leopard is fast, and from the racket behind us, it's utterly decimating the treasure room as it passes through. Guilt flashes through me—a museum would kill for just one of those priceless artifacts. Oh, well. It's the least of our concerns.

The cat appears behind us and Ryan sends another arrow into it.

I make the mistake of looking back to watch its flight. My toe snags a loose tile and I go down hard, the scythe clattering out of my grip.

Ryan skids to a stop, his bow up, but the leopard is upon me.

I just manage to get the shield up in time, hiding my torso and head behind it.

The leopard scrabbles at the shield with its raking claws, its snarling maw filling my vision. Its weight on top of me is suffocating; I think my ribs might break from the pressure. One of its stone hind legs steps on my ankle and I scream as the creature's sharp claws pierce my skin. A horrible though occurs to me. Do seers see their own deaths? Maybe the magic doesn't work that way. Maybe Ryan and I both die here, but I just didn't realize…

Two more arrows bury themselves in the leopard's face as it claws at me, and I see in my darkening vision the scythe swinging towards the leopard's head. Warning rings in my mind. What if the scythe breaks on the stone, and we'll never be free of the curse? But something else happens. The weight upon me disappears and a cloud of sand rains down upon me.

I gag and cough, brushing the sand out of my eyes, my mouth.

"What—?" I begin to ask.

"Get up," Ryan's voice is insistent.

I scramble to my feet, my ankle screaming in protest, and register our predicament. The scythe somehow dispatched the leopard, but the other creatures have caught up. Dog, centaur, gryphon. It's three against two. Or, I reassess, with the dog's three heads, maybe more like five. The centaur looses an arrow towards Ryan and I heave the shield in front of him, acting on instinct.

The bolt twangs into the metal, vibrating.

I take the scythe from Ryan, freeing his arms for his bow. He has an arrow nocked and flying at the centaur before I even swing the scythe at the creatures. The stone animals shy back. Clearly, the scythe can hurt them. Turn them back into the dust from whence they came. Good to know it still has some juice—not that it gets us any closer to figuring out how the hell to break the curse.

Ryan lets an arrow fly and it knocks the centaur's bow from its hand. "Run," he growls, and we launch into action.

My lungs feel compressed, each heaving breath sending shooting pain through me. Wet blood drips into my boot, and pain radiates through my ankle. I think the leopard might have crushed some of the bones. Stark reality slams into place. I can't outrun them. Not like this.

"In here," Ryan says, ducking through a side door. There's an actual door here attached to this opening—thick timber vanished to a shine. We heave it shut, and blessed gods, there's a sturdy piece of wood to bar it closed. Ryan throws the crossbar down just as one of the stone creatures hurls itself against the door.

We both step back from the thudding on the other side of the door. Tears prick my eyes from the pain of every step—every breath.

"That's not going to buy us much time," Ryan says. "We have to get the hell out of here." He only has three more arrows in his quiver.

I turn to survey our surroundings, and my mouth goes dry. It's a long, rectangular room flanked by columns. I recognize this room. This is the room where Ryan dies.

CHAPTER 31

"We have to get the hell out of here," I say, my voice twisting and shrill.

"That's what I just sai—" Ryan cuts himself off when he sees my face. He pales as he comprehends what I realized. "Oh."

A ferocious thud against the door startles me free of the suffocating pull of the vision, and I shake my head. "The scythe can kill them. We can do this."

"So you want to make a stand?" he asks. I can tell he thinks this is a terrible idea. That this is how he dies. He's probably right. One scythe, three monsters. Not great odds.

"Maybe there's something else here," I say, feeling panic and pain curl the edges of my mind, tinting everything red. I limp across the room, examining the dark recesses between the columns. There's nothing. Nothing except... "Oh my god."

Sitting quietly in the corner of the room, hidden behind the row of columns, is the largest loom I have ever seen.

"Ryan, come here." I motion him over, and he jogs to my side, looking over his shoulder warily at the shuddering door. Dust rains down from the frame each time a beast throws itself against the wood. There's no way the door will hold for long. They'll break through the wall itself at this rate.

"Is that…" His blue eyes go wide.

"The loom of the Three Fates."

"I hate those bitches." Ryan shakes his head darkly.

"Me too!" I say, amazed that we've only just discovered this kinship. "The Fates weave the tapestry of all life on Earth. Each thread is a life." The pattern is magnificent, the cloth as long as Ryan's truck is lengthwise. But it's the colors that really astound me. There must be thousands of hues—rainbows of color, swirls and starbursts of interconnected lives.

"But the Fates aren't even here anymore? How is it still working?" Ryan asks.

Ryan is right. Even as we stand there, the shuttle moves ever so slightly, a line of threads creeping infinitesimally forwards.

"How is any of this still here?" I shrug helplessly.

"I guess physical objects were more permanent than the gods themselves. Sibyll was right."

I'm drawn to a warp in the fabric, where a few threads are tangled. I step in closer and lean until my nose is almost touching the fabric, examining the threads. What happened here? My eyes widen in recognition as I see the threads. Two of them have been cut, but they're held into the fabric by the tight hold of the neighboring threads—the knotted tangle.

"Sweet baby Jesus, I know how to break the curse," I say, breathless.

"How?" Ryan's face is before mine in an instant. "Don't mess with me."

"This tangle. This is us! Look. There are eight threads. Seven Pleiades sisters, one for Orion. Two have been cut.

Those are Electra and Alcyone, who've died in this lifetime. Look! If you trace the threads back…" I move farther up the loom until I'm standing on my tippy-toes pointing to another tangle. "Same threads. Six of them have been cut here. But because of the tangle, they're stuck in the fabric."

"Gods, Mer, you're right," Ryan breathes.

"If I use the scythe to cut and untangle the threads, it should break the curse, right?"

"It's as good a guess as any. What's the worst that could happen?"

"I could cut all our threads and we'd all die and our souls would be lost forever," I suggest.

The wood splinters on the door across the room, and the sharp beak of the gryphon comes snapping through, a piercing cry escaping from its mouth.

Crap. I take the scythe, frowning at its unwieldy bulk. The thing is made for harvesting grain, not cutting delicate threads as thin as spider silk. "I wish this thing were a pair of scissors," I grumble, turning to the task at hand.

The scythe transforms in my hand. Into a pair of scissors.

"Hey, awesome!" I hold it up to Ryan, delighted.

"How'd you do that?" Ryan asks.

"I just told it I wished it were scissors."

At the far end of the room, the door explodes inwards off its hinges, and the gryphon skids across the floor, its wicked talons digging grooves into the stone floor.

Ryan yanks the scissors out of my hand. "I wish you were an arrow!" In one lithe motion, he knocks the transformed scythe against his string and lets loose. It pierces the gryphon straight in the chest and the creature disintegrates into a cloud of sand.

"Well, I need it back now," I say, panicked. The arrow is now lying on the ground all the way across the room.

"I'll get it." Ryan groans, then runs straight at the approaching Cerberus statue.

I turn to the knot, examining it. At least I can be ready and know what to do when he returns. I realize that the two loose threads of my sisters who've died are already free. Could I...tie them back together? I lean in, and ever so carefully, extract from the tangle one of the purple threads that I know is Electra. Then I pull the other one, and, thanking my Girl Scout days, tie them gently together in a knot. The thread vibrates, a golden charge running up and down its length. I release it in alarm and when I lean back in to examine what's happened, I see. The thread is whole once more. Healed.

I let out a gasp of relief and grab eagerly for other cut thread—the goldenrod. Ryan bellows in pain and I look over my shoulder to see the three-headed dog on top of him, Ryan's forearm in one of its mouths.

"Ryan!" I scream, horror filling me as another head snaps for Ryan's throat. But the creature turns to dust and I spot the scythe-turned-dagger in Ryan's fist.

I sag in relief and turn back to the loom, pulling Alcyone's threads and tying them quickly.

Ryan limps to my side, his mangled arm cradled to his chest. I try not to think about how it looks just like the injury from my vision.

"Where's the centaur?" I ask.

"Don't know." Ryan hands the scythe to me, and it transforms back into the shears. His face is sweaty and smeared with dust and blood, but in that moment, he's never looked more devastatingly handsome.

My heart squeezes painfully as I turn back to the loom. "Keep an eye out."

"I don't know if I can pull the bow right now. If it comes, I'll need the scythe," he replies.

"Okay." I turn back to the task at hand, examining the threads before me. The remaining ones are in a tangle. I squint, trying to trace their paths, to see which one needs to be cut next. I recognize the forest green one as Ryan's. It's twined around a sky-blue thread that I see is mine. It's farther outside the knot, threading only through Ryan's. His is hopelessly tangled with the others. I squint, cocking my head. The green thread runs down, around the magenta and purple—but those would untwine if it were freed… My mind works on the pattern until my eyes widen in recognition. In horror.

Ryan's anguished scream breaks my concentration and I look up with startled attention, coming back to the room. There's a stone arrow protruding from Ryan's shoulder.

"Ryan!" I screech and start towards him, but an arrow flies towards me, and I shy out of its way, back behind the pillars by the loom. The centaur is back. Apparently, he went to reload.

"Pass me the scythe, Mer," Ryan says quietly as the centaur notches another arrow and lets it fly.

Ryan tries to dodge, but he's too slow. It buries itself into his thigh. A cry of agony rips from him, twisting me in knots. He falls to his knees, doubled over in pain.

I return to the loom, releasing a shuddering breath, my hands shaking over the threads. Over the green thread. Once again, Ryan's life is in my hands. One little snip is all it'll take to end it.

"Mer!" he cries, desperate for the weapon. I look back and see the centaur approaching slowly, another arrow ready. Its hooves echo on the floor. *Clop. Clop.*

If I'm to give Ryan a prayer of a chance of defending himself, I have to throw him the scythe now. But I can't. Because I need to use it to snip the green thread. It's the only way to end this. It's his life that's desperately intertwined, warping the threads around it. If I use the scythe to cut his thread, my sisters' and my threads will untangle. We'll be free. The curse will be broken.

"Now, Mer," he pleads. Ryan is on his knees, his hand outstretched towards me, his fingers grasping. The centaur is upon him, standing tall before him, its bow pointed towards his chest. It looks like an execution. His wild, blue eyes meet mine, and I let myself drown in them one last time.

I'm sorry, I mouth as I look away. For I cannot face the moment when he realizes what I'm about to do. I'm too much of a coward.

I can barely see the pattern through my refracted tears. I trace the emerald thread with shaking fingers. I slip the shears underneath the delicate filament and close my eyes.

Snip.

CHAPTER 32

The threads begin to right themselves as Ryan's slips free of the knot. But now it's slipping farther, the blunt end of the emerald filament pulling itself from the fabric. I lunge at it, grabbing the two loose ends with delicate fingers, holding it steady. "Oh no, you don't," I mutter. I try to ignore that Ryan looks exactly like I saw him in my vision. But I didn't see the loom in my vision. I didn't know about this chance.

The sound of hoofbeats striking stone startles me and I throw a look over my shoulder. Ryan's body has gone still; no hint of breath moves his chest. The centaur has lowered its bow. It has no interest in dispatching dead intruders. That's not what the spell raised it to do.

But not every intruder is dead.

The centaur's gaze swings to me. *Shit.*

I move on instinct, transferring the two tiny threads to one hand, freeing my other to seize the scythe-scissors. And then I throw those suckers with every ounce of strength in this mortal body.

The scissors sail through the air, borne on my fevered prayers, and bury themselves in the centaur's chest.

"Yes!" I whoop as the centaur explodes into dust, raining down upon Ryan's still form.

Ryan.

I turn back to the loom, to the two precious threads held in my hand. The pattern of my sisters' threads is beautiful—a riot of color woven together in perfect harmony. Seven threads, a rainbow of colors. Lives well-lived. I find the tiny vacancy where Ryan's thread should lie. I look at the pattern, uncertain. Yes, it should be woven under mine, and looped around once.

I hesitate. Is it wrong to keep him tied to me like that? Even though it's what I desperately want? But it's what the Fates ordained, what the warp and weft of the fabric is calling for. To hold us apart would be to break the pattern. And the Fates must have had some wisdom, after all.

I carefully thread Ryan's filament around mine before tying it off delicately. My soul is keening within me. This must work. If this doesn't work, it will break me. I've seen much of death in my many lives, but never have I caused it. I suddenly understand the yoke of guilt that Ryan must have carried all of these years, all these lives. If this doesn't work…

Ryan's green thread vibrates and a shimmer of gold runs up and down its length. I pull my hand back with a gasp, and then look closely at the fabric. The pattern is perfect.

A groan behind me makes my heart leap. I whirl around. Ryan is stirring, leaning on one elbow, brushing centaur sand out of his hair.

"I've died a lot of times," he croaks. "But that was one of the worst."

I run to his side and fall to my knees beside him, helping him sit up.

"Your arm," I say, marveling. The wound from the Cerberus dog, the arrow in his shoulder—he's healed.

My wounds rush back in sharp and angry—the throbbing pain in my ankle, the vise grip of my ribs around my lungs.

"My girlfriend snipped my lifeline and all I got for it was this healed body," he says with a wry grin.

Hope surges in me. That he's not angry. That I haven't ruined everything by sacrificing him. "Girlfriend?" I ask, unable to keep the answering smile from my face.

"The couple that slays together stays together," he says, still through that ridiculous grin.

"Are you just going to keep the idioms up or are you going to kiss me?"

"No more idioms." He leans in, pressing his mouth to mine.

Grains of sand cling to his full lips, but nothing short of another invasion by ancient Grecian attack statues could make me break off this kiss. He threads his hand in my hair and I wrap my arms around his shoulders, pressing my chest to his, ignoring my protesting ribs. He tastes of bacon and coffee and destiny.

We drown in each other for a time, reveling in our newfound freedom, in each other. His lips move against mine in a way that steals my good sense and sends heat coiling through this teenage body. No—my body. For I'm finally just me. Meriah.

Eventually, I come up for air, pulling back. Ryan gently kisses the tip of my nose and each of my eyelids before pulling me into a hug. He feels so warm and good and *alive* that I can't stop the emotion from flooding over me.

"I'm so sorry, Ryan," I say. "It was the only way. I didn't want to do it, but your thread was what was holding the others out of place—"

"Shh," he murmurs into my hair. "I came here expecting

to die. But you saved me. I'm here—whole. Curse-free. That's what I choose to remember."

I look into his eyes, uncertain. "So you…forgive me?"

"For cutting my thread? Of course. For kidnapping me and holding me hostage without even anything to watch on TV…? That's going to take some serious groveling on your part."

I shove him with a laugh.

He gets to his feet and offers me his hands. "Let's get the hell out of here."

Ryan pulls me up, and I hiss as I put weight on my injured ankle. He retrieves his bow and arrows, the scythe, and the shield. "In case we encounter anything else on the way out."

"You think there might be something else?" My eyes go wide.

"No, of course not."

"You're a terrible liar." I groan.

"Takes one to know one," he shoots back.

Ain't that the truth.

I put my arm around Ryan's shoulder and we start slowly towards the exit.

We aren't even out of the loom's chamber when Ryan frowns. "The key is tugging at me."

"Maybe it's showing us a shortcut?" I offer hopefully. It's going to take forever to get out of here at this rate, and I'm eager to be gone from this place. The sibyl's warning is loud in my mind. The stone creatures might not be the only trap here.

"Maybe."

"It didn't lead us astray before. Let's follow it."

We turn around and start towards the exit at the back of the room. Ryan huffs, and before I know it, he's scooping me up into his arms. "Hey!" I protest. "I can walk."

"I know you can," he says. "But it'll be faster this way."

The pain of his grip on my ribs is powerful, but it's a dull roar compared to the fireworks that were going off in my ankle. "My hero," I say in a simpering voice.

"I think you're the hero in this one. You figured out the loom. You broke the curse."

I lean my head against his shoulder, weariness washing over me. "We can both be the hero."

"How very progressive of us."

"What can I say? We're that kind of ancient reincarnated couple."

"Not anymore," he says. "We're just normal teenagers now."

I sigh happily. "Normal. Normal sounds good."

"Normal sounds perfect."

The key does, in fact, lead us to another exit from Olympus. I guess it makes sense that there's more than one way in and out of this place.

Ryan sets me down and slips the key into the lock. I expect for some sort of warning klaxon to sound when he does, but Olympus stays silent and still. I guess we passed its test, and it's content to let us go.

Our passage through the Byway has none of the clinging suspense of our last trip. We aren't frightened kids unsure of what we'll face inside Olympus. We're conquering heroes, curse vanquishers. But mostly, we're just dirty and tired and seriously jonesing for a cheeseburger.

Stepping from the dim fog of the Byway into the brilliant sunshine of Shasta's afternoon is startling. I hold up a hand against the sun, letting my pupils adjust. I heave a sigh as Ryan pulls the key out of the lock and the portal closes behind us. I can't believe we frickin' did it!

"Mer," Ryan whispers, nudging me with his elbow and nodding a ways down the hill.

I squint until two figures come into view in the meadow

below us. Between Brandon's signature curls and Zoe's black hair shining almost blue in the sun, there's no question who it is. Despite the fact that the two are having a serious make-out sesh in the wildflowers.

I press my lips together, trying to keep the grin from my face. *Go Zoe!*

"Come on," Ryan mouths, and we creep down the hill, as quiet as mice—well, a limping mouse for me.

When we're standing just feet from where Brandon is lying on top of Zoe, kissing the living daylights out of her, Ryan clears his throat.

Zoe screeches and the two fly apart.

Ryan crosses his arms before his chest. "So just how long exactly did you mourn your dead friend before you made your move on Zoe?"

The relief on Brandon's face at the sight of Ryan is palpable.

"Mer?" Zoe wipes her mouth, trying to smooth her hair. It's hopeless. She still looks well and thoroughly kissed. "Did you do it? Did you break the curse?"

Ryan and I just look at each other and grin.

CHAPTER 33

The soft May breeze tousles my hair through the truck's open window. My face is raised to the sun, basking in its warmth. Ryan's and my fingers are threaded together on the bench seat between us. We're driving to Sibyll's house to return the key and the other items that we took from Olympus.

Ryan and I debated what to do over the past three weeks. We have the scythe, the shield, and his bow and arrows. All are precious relics that would garner a small fortune at a sale to a museum or private collector. We could use that money, Ryan especially. But with all our good fortune, it doesn't seem right to keep them. Sibyll will know what to do.

The drive back from Shasta was ebullient. It took some serious doing to get me down the mountain back to camp, but between Ryan and Brandon, we managed. The guys packed up camp while Zoe and I engaged in some covert squealing, and she told me every whispered detail of what had happened with Brandon. Sometimes a comforting hug over shared sorrow turns into something more. I couldn't be happier for Zo. The two of them have been inseparable the last few weeks. I have to admit they make a perfect couple.

I got some serious lectures about safety when I returned from camping—it turned out I had two fractured ribs and a broken ankle from my "fall" on the "hiking trail." Track season was over for me, and I'd have some physical therapy to do—but I didn't mind spending my time curled on the couch with Ryan binging Netflix shows.

Ryan looks over at me and I smile at him. I find us doing that a lot. There's an inordinate amount of looking and smiling. And kissing. Gods, is there a lot of kissing. I can't seem to get enough. The song on the radio changes and Ryan and I both tap our feet to the twanging country beat. I'm not sure I've ever felt so free. Ryan hasn't had a seizure since we got back—not even a headache. I haven't had a vision. I think we're finally free.

And then there's my sisters—Alcyone, who died after nearly drowning, and Electra, who died in the car crash. When we returned, the news had changed. We could find no sign that either girl had ever died—both walked away from their accidents safe and whole. Deputy Romano was nowhere to be found, either. No investigation. No warrant. Even the subtle warp in Ryan's fender had disappeared. I guess tying those threads together changed the fabric of reality, too.

Ryan pulls into Sibyll's driveway, and the shimmering ribbon of the river doesn't send fear stabbing into me this time. We called ahead this time around.

We gather our ancient artifacts and I can tell we're a little hesitant to see them go. To release the stories they represented.

"Ready?" Ryan asks.

I shrug. "Ready as I'll ever be."

Sibyll opens the door before we can knock. She's excited.

"Come in! I can't wait to see what you brought." Her eyes caress the gemstone-encrusted shield as I carry it past her, and I can tell she's dying to hold it.

She offers us our choice of LaCroix and we accept, laying down everything on the coffee table.

Ryan wraps his arm around my shoulder and I settle against his side on the couch.

Sibyll puts her glasses on and inspects everything, marveling at the craftsmanship, the detail. We filled her in on our trip through Olympus over the phone, so all there is to do is return the artifacts and the key.

Finally, she puts the scythe down. It's still in scissor form. "You can make it turn into a scythe if you want," I explain, taking it and willing it to change form. When it transforms once more into a curved blade with a long, wooden handle, she lets out a surprised little screech, falling back on the couch.

"Marvelous." Sibyll presses a hand to her chest, letting out a shaky breath. "I've talked to the other sibyls about what's to be done."

Ryan and I exchange a look. That sounds ominous.

"We're in agreement that the scythe is too powerful to fall into mortal hands. The order of the sibyls will hide it and keep it safe."

I nod. That's a reasonable precaution.

"As to the other items, they belong in a museum. We've reached out to a few contacts, and there's a lot of interest. We'll be setting up an auction. The sibyls also agree that the bow and arrows belong to you, Ryan. Any amount we get for their sale is yours."

We exchanged another glance. That's surprisingly fair.

"How much do you think you'll get for them?" he asks nonchalantly, but his fingers tighten on mine.

"At least two million."

"Two—million—" Ryan splutters. Warmth floods me. This could change everything for Ryan.

I wrap his torso in a hug and he rests his chin on my head, squeezing me back. "What about the shield?" he asks.

"The shield will likely garner a larger price due to the precious gemstones inlaid in its surface. At least ten million."

Zeus's balls, that's a lot of money.

"The sibyls agree that it's appropriate for us to award Meriah a finder's fee for her role in retrieving the shield from Olympus. It was no easy feat."

"How much?" I ask. Now it's my turn to pretend to be nonchalant.

"Ten percent," she says, and my mouth drops open. A million dollars.

"I hope this is acceptable to both of you. The sibyls will retain the remainder of the proceeds to continue to fund our work."

We both nod. I take a gulp of my LaCroix. I'm suddenly feeling parched.

The rest of our meeting is a blur. All Ryan and I can see are dollar signs. What we could do with that money. A newer house for his grandma to live in. Care for her when she needs it. College—without student loan debt.

We walk back out into the bright sunshine, waving goodbye to Sibyll. She's suggested that Ryan and I consider degrees in history. We already have the background.

Ryan opens my door, helping me into the truck as the orthopedic boot on my foot is unwieldy.

He closes the door and comes around the other side, hopping in. The truck roars to life.

"I was thinking about what she said," Ryan says as he backs down her driveway.

"You want to be a historian?" I arch a brow. I'm sure Ryan could do anything he put his mind to, but I can't really see him holed up in a dusty library. Though he would look cute in one of those blazers with the leather arm patches.

"No. But maybe…an archeologist." He puts the truck into drive. "Being out in the field… I don't know. It's not a very practical career."

"I think it's perfect," I say, and I do. "Besides, you've got two million reasons why you don't have to be practical."

He lets out a delighted laugh. "Come 'ere."

I scoot across the seat and into his open arms.

"I don't mind the money, but there's really one true prize I got out of all of this. You." He kisses the top of my head.

"Samesies," I say as I burrow into his side. I was a seer for a hundred lifetimes, and even I couldn't have foreseen how perfectly everything would unfold. How it would all bring us here to this. Happiness. Maybe the Fates aren't such bitches after all.

THE END

ABOUT THE AUTHOR

Claire Luana grew up in Seattle reading everything she could get her hands on and writing every chance she could. Eventually, adulthood won out, and she turned her writing talents to more scholarly pursuits, going to work as a commercial litigation attorney.

While continuing to practice law, Claire decided to return to her roots and try her hand once again at creative writing. She has written and published the four fantasy series: the Moonburner Cycle, the Confectioner Chronicles, the Knights of Caerleon, co-written with Jesikah Sundin, and The Faerie Race, co-written with J.A. Armitage.

She lives in Seattle, Washington with her husband and two dogs. In her (little) remaining spare time, she loves to hike, travel, binge-watch CW shows, and of course, fall into a good book.

Connect with Claire Luana online at www.claireluana.com

facebook.com/claireluana

twitter.com/clairedeluana

instagram.com/claireluana

goodreads.com/ClaireLuana

amazon.com/author/claireluana

bookbub.com/authors/claireluana